THE

BLACK MASS

J. D. FORTIER

ISBN: 978-0-9939338-3-7

DEDICATION

I dedicate this novel to my editor Kristy-Lynn Hankerwitz of the GTA, who devoted many hours to editing and polishing this book, readying it for publishing. I would also like to thank Debra Kirvan, Bryan Minnes my good friends for their support and encouragement to keep writing.

INTRODUCTION

This story came to me through a dream.

I have always been fascinated by the idea of other realities beyond our familiar world.

Jenna Paxton's the protagonist is beset with insecurities and fears from a young age. Abandoned by her parents and raise by an acquaintance of her mother's, she grows up with low esteem and difficulties with relationships, particularly intimate ones with men.

Encouraged and supported by her best friend Andrea, Jenna slowly learns to believe in herself. As Jenna rebuilds and shapes a future, he is becoming happy, even content, but then people dearest to her suddenly start disappearing and dying.

A paranormal thriller, this book is full of intrigue, mystery, and human fear of the unknown. It will lift you from this mundane world of everyday existence into a faraway, enigmatic sphere.

You never know who will be next . . .

CHAPTER ONE

Andrea jolted up drenched in a cold sweat. *Not again!* She thought. The bed looked as if she had fought in a battle during the night. The sheets and covers were a bundled-up mess, and the pillows were on the floor. She laid still for a few minutes, trying to calm her breathing.

"When is this going to stop?" she angrily said out loud, flinging the crumpled sheets onto the floor. Waking up each morning lately meant having to get through yet another day dealing with her unsettled thoughts about her friend, Jenna. Each night in her dreams, Andrea relived the scene at the lake where she made her desperate plea to Jenna. *"No, no, don't go, it's not real. Please, listen to me!"* It was a terrifying experience, and most mornings, Andrea struggled with her emotions, trying to make sense of Jenna's unforeseen departure.

For months, Andrea continued to wonder about Jenna's destiny. Still dazed by what she had witnessed, Andrea searched for answers at the library. The question that plagued her most was about Jenna's path in this life. Was her life on earth predestined from a previous lifetime, but unknown to her conscious mind?

Although Jenna was an attractive woman with shoulder-length auburn hair, she lacked self-confidence, and her self-image was poor. She was never comfortable with who she was, and being assertive in a relationship caused her much anxiety, especially when it came to having relationships with men.

When Jenna first dated and then married Gary, and the same thing later occurred with Brandon, there was an underlying vagueness about both relationships that troubled Jenna, but she chose to ignore it. Another question Andrea kept asking was whether these two relationships were meant to test Jenna in some way.

Although Jenna truly loved Gary, their marriage seemed strained at times, due to his lack of communication with her about important issues. He always avoided conversation when it came to more serious matters, and he would go off into a world of his own and she wouldn't see him for hours at times. Andrea recalled a conversation she had with Jenna about Gary and Brandon's strange ways; it was Brandon's odd mannerisms that bothered Jenna the most.

"Brandon is more interesting than Gary was," she weakly remarked. "We have a few of the same interests, but there is an aspect about his character that puzzles me" she said anxiously.

Andrea remembered blankly staring at Jenna for a few minutes, wondering if she was beginning to feel fearful again, a prevailing characteristic of her past. It had taken Andrea quite a while to convince Jenna to think more positively about relationships and that she deserved to be loved.

Andrea's large, five-foot-eight frame and bright red hair made Jenna's five-foot-four look tiny in comparison, plus Andrea didn't hesitate to say what was on her mind, and she could be forceful with her words when the occasion called for it.

"If there are things about him that bother you, tell him how you feel," Andrea said, clearly making her point.

Jenna became sullen. "I've tried, but each time I start to say something, he looks at me as if I'm the one whose has the problem, and I clam up."

"Then why do you keep seeing him if he makes you feel uncomfortable?" Andrea asked defiantly.

"I've asked myself that question a few times. I don't know why. Maybe because we have a few things in common, and I don't exactly go out there to meet men now, do I? That's true. But if it were me, I wouldn't hesitate to ask him some questions. Especially if I felt the way you do."

"I know, but I'm not you," Jenna said, frustrated.

"No, you're not like me. But you need to either accept him as he is or stop going out with him," Andrea said getting a little impatient with Jenna.

Feeling annoyed, Jenna countered, "That's easy for you to say."

It seemed that Jenna was beset with insecurities and fears right from her birth. Her father had left her family when she was a baby, and when Jenna was four years old, her mother abandoned her as well, and she was left to be raised by an acquaintance of her mother's. Although the woman took Jenna in, she had a drinking problem that affected her ability to nurture Jenna as she should have been able to.

Jenna struggled throughout her teens, dealing with her unresolved emotional issues. She didn't feel worthy enough to be loved. Consequently, as Jenna grew older, it became increasingly difficult for her to trust those who claimed they cared for her, and because she had been deserted, her feelings of rejection and distrust progressed. These feelings intensified, especially whenever relationships with men became more intimate.

The people who knew Jenna best tried to make her feel better by telling her she deserved a loving relationship, and that it wasn't her fault her parents had forsaken her. She dismissed all efforts of encouragement until she met Andrea at work.

Andrea worked as a counsellor for underprivileged children, and Jenna was an assistant, helping her with the problematic children. They became good friends. Up to that point, Jenna had preferred being alone.

Andrea came from a solid family background. Her parents always encouraged her to use her talents and skills, and she was self-assured and confident. After obtaining a good education, she chose a career as a counsellor helping underprivileged children. Her abilities, courage and strength were the catalysts from which Jenna finally gained trust, love, and encouragement, giving her confidence to move forward with her life in a more positive way. With Andrea's support, Jenna found the courage to choose another career that she liked better, and she became an associate editor for a new publishing company.

Jenna and Gary dated for about a year before they decided to get married. There were together only two years when one day, an environmental associate of Gary's called Jenna to say she had bad news.

"I'm so sorry to tell you this, Jenna, but I just heard that Gary died suddenly while he was working on a project. He was carrying out some studies in a field in one of the rural districts in Alberta, when he fell to the ground."

Jenna wasn't really hearing the words. She felt numb, but Gary's associate kept talking. "A man walking his dog in the area saw him fall. He checked Gary's pulse, but couldn't feel any beat. There were no visible injuries that he could see, but he noticed an unusual black mass hovering over where Gary lay. The rest of the sky was blue with no other clouds in sight. He called for an ambulance, and Gary's body was taken to the nearest hospital and pronounced dead upon arrival." Complete silence followed for a few minutes after the associate finished her spiel.

"Jenna, did you hear me, are you still there?"

Shocked, Jenna had slumped down on the sofa holding the phone in her hand. With tears rolling down her cheeks, she wailed, "Gary is . . . dead. Oh, my God! I can't talk right now," and she slammed the phone down.

Later, a newspaper reporter wrote about the incident and mentioned that the man who found the body told the reporter the details of what he saw. "When I got close to the man's body an eerie black fog hovered over him as he lay there. I was stumped by the strange incident and couldn't make heads or tails of what the black fog could have been."

Upon completion of the coroner's examination, it was recorded that the cause of Gary's sudden demise was an unusual circumstance of cardiac arrest. There were no physical injuries on his body that indicated foul play. Both the doctor and the coroner were puzzled by the case. The doctor commented to Jenna that in his entire medical career, he had never come across this type of medical anomaly.

* * *

It was in the summer of 2000 when Jenna first noticed Gary. He was working on a project near the building where she worked. The first time she set eyes on him, he was standing outside without a shirt on, near a vacant lot adjacent to a building next to her place of employment, the publishing company. He scratched his head and mumbled out loud,

15

appearing to be in a quandary about something. Jenna and Andrea usually met up at break-time, and they were outside when Jenna first saw him.

She guessed he was in his late forties or early fifties, and she was astounded by his muscular physique. Splatters of peppery white strands on his temples stuck out like cropped porcupine quills against his dark, wavy brown hair. His appearance got her attention; she liked the way he looked.

Andrea egged her on: "I dare you. Go have a chat with him. This is your chance. Look at him. Wow!" But Jenna didn't approach him that day.

Another day, while Gary removed some planks from a truck, she finally found the nerve to talk to him after another co-worker's persistence.

She walked up to him and, nervously extending her hand out, said, "Hi, my name is Jenna Paxton. I work in the building next door. You must be new to this area."

Shaking her hand firmly, he replied, "Hi, Gary Thompson. Yes, I just moved here from Labrador about a month ago, I got a job working for the environmental department for a company called 'A Green Earth,' two weeks ago, there are always environmental issues in this province, and I was hired to try and fix some of these problems. How about you, what do you do?"

"I'm an associate editor for the magazine company in the building next to where you work." She pointed to her building. "I work with new authors helping them to market their books."

"That sounds like an interesting job."

"I enjoy it," Jenna responded, pretending to be forthright.

"I need a coffee. Would you care to join me at the bistro across the way?" he asked her as he fixed his eyes upon her.

Smiling, she replied, "Sure, why not, I could use a good cup of coffee right about now," she said, as she examined more closely.

They walked to the bistro, ordered a coffee and a donut each, and sat down to continue their conversation. From the onset of their first meeting, Gary seemed different from any of the other men Jenna had dated. His humour was dry, sometimes even witty, yet there seemed to be a certain restraint about his personality that she found inexplicable.

After that initial meeting, they had dated for five months, and their union deepened. He was a sensual and caring lover, and she really liked that about him. They enjoyed outdoor activities, playing tennis, going to the movies, and just being together. Their sexual intimacy was very satisfying to her, something she had never experienced with other men. They were very happy and planned to marry.

● * *

After Gary's death, as the months went by, Jenna couldn't stop thinking about the mystery that surrounded his sudden passing. She was emotionally crushed.

Not once did she recall him complaining about any health issues. As far as she knew, he was completely healthy. They were together for over two years; she would have noticed if anything were wrong.

Despite what the doctor told her, something didn't feel right about the circumstances that surrounded Gary's death, and she continued inquiring into his past activities. However, after many months of speaking to different people and asking numerous questions, she was no further ahead in finding out any details that helped her to understand the circumstances better.

During the time, they were together, they had planned on having children. Unfortunately, they were told that Gary was sterile, and they had made the decision to adopt. The papers were ready to be signed when she found out about Gary's death and her life came crashing down like a concrete wall.

Although devastated, she was grateful for her position as an associate editor. It kept her busy, helping her not to think about Gary and the eerie event. Her profession then became her life.

CHAPTER TWO

A little over a year after Gary's demise, Andrea, her best friend, insisted that Jenna check the Internet for a reputable online dating service. "Come on, Jenna check them out. It's been long enough that you have been alone; it's time."

Wrinkling her nose, Jenna said, "A dating service?! Uh-Uh. No, I don't think so! I know of a couple of situations that turned out to be pretty frightening for the women."

"They're not all bad. You just need to do research. Find a service with a good reputation, one that requires more references."

Jenna hesitatingly grabbed the mouse, still unsure. But after considering Andrea's suggestion, she finally looked at some profiles on different dating services; no one caught her immediate attention.

"I'll try one more time. If I don't see someone who strikes my fancy, then I'll forget about it."

"You have nothing to lose. You never know, there might be someone there when you least expect it."

A month had gone by since she first searched online dating services when she received an email from a dating service saying they interviewed a man who they thought might be a good fit for her.

When Andrea asked Jenna if she contacted the man the agency had suggested, Jenna's eyebrows lifted and she replied, "I haven't responded yet."

"They're not going to come knocking on your door, Jenna. Take the initiative. Go for it!"

"OK, OK, I will, just to get you off my back."

Not long after, Jenna replied to the e-mail. A woman from the dating service arranged to introduce the man to Jenna over dinner at a local restaurant. It was the agency's policy for someone from the agency to be at the first meeting, to get a better sense of their personalities. Nevertheless, it didn't lead to any more dates with that man. She wasn't impressed.

Jenna's friends and co-workers tried to get her to move on with her life, initiating her to look at dating services and to go out to bars, but Jenna wasn't interested.

Then one morning during a coffee break, Stacey, a tall attractive co-worker, approached Jenna. "I'm planning on having a few people over for dinner tonight, would you like to join us?" she asked.

Jenna was uncertain, but she said, "Yes, that would be nice, thank you. What time should I be there?"

"Come around 6:30. We'll have a drink before dinner. There's someone I would like you to meet."

Concerned Jenna said, "I see. A setup, huh?"

"No, not a setup. It will be fine. He's a friend of my boyfriend. I thought you might enjoy his company. He's interesting, fun, likes to try new things. Don't you think you've been alone long enough?

Sighing, Jenna reluctantly said, "I'm not really sure if I am ready to meet anyone yet, Stacey."

"You have to let go of the past so you can move forward. Constantly mulling over things from the past is not doing you any good, be done with it. You can't change what happened. You did all you could. Start enjoying your life again!"

"You're probably right. OK. I'll give it a whirl."

"Great. I'll see you at 6:30." Stacey replied, but then thought maybe she should have left well enough alone.

As Jenna walked into Stacey's living room that evening, the man was quick to get up and shake her hand, "Hi, Brandon Styles; It's a pleasure to meet you."

Stiffening up, Jenna said, "Jenna Paxton. Nice to meet you, too."

Brandon's handshake felt taut, and it made her hand prickle. He was tall like Gary, but not handsome in the knock-your-socks-off good looks kind of way; his appearance was more along the line of Clint Eastwood's. There was an aspect of his personality she couldn't quite describe. He seemed unusually reserved, and there were moments when he'd stare right past her as though she wasn't in the room.

He said he enjoyed going to movie theatres, dining out, and walking on nature trails. His favorite pastime was sailing. It seemed that they shared a few interests.

Later in the week, Jenna bumped into Brandon while attending a conference organized by a magazine company she liked. The company had placed an article in the newspaper about some of the growing economic issues in Calgary, Alberta, and Brandon was particularly interested in hearing what they had to say. He made a point of speaking to Jenna about the lack of support for a better way of promoting affordable housing. Her interest in him continued to mount. The conference was a weekend event and over dinner one evening, he asked her out on a date. "Would you consider going to a movie with me tomorrow night?"

"Yes, I'd like that. What kind of movies do you like?" she asked.

"I am quite fond of the old classics."

Her eyes widening, she said, "Really? That's interesting, so do I!"

"That's great," he said with a slightly awkward grin. "How about we have a bite to eat and then take in a movie? I'll pick you up at around 6:00."

"That sounds like fun."

Jenna wasn't one-hundred percent certain about dating Brandon, mostly because he was ten years older than she was.

She wondered if she really wanted to be with someone that much older than her, but the more she thought about it, she decided she shouldn't make that kind of judgement without knowing that much about him.

Overall, their first date was a success. They liked each other, and they agreed to meet again in a week's time. He suggested seeing a play for their next date, which was an activity Jenna also enjoyed.

From that day forward, as Jenna and Brandon continued to date, they spent time walking along nature trails and dining out at different restaurants, where she noted his peculiarity regarding certain foods. He was totally appalled by dishes that included meats, foul, or fish. He wouldn't eat anything that included animals or sea bearing creatures. He ate only vegetables. She questioned him why he was so against meats and foul; he just said he preferred not to eat foods that were made from creatures, and nothing more was said about the subject.

They both enjoyed antiques, ancient history books, and old LP records. Other interests of his included travelling to different towns, exploring the sights, and sailing.

Brandon was a good conversationalist, but he didn't care to talk about his past. In the early stages of their relationship, she thought it was odd, and as their relationship intensified, Jenna didn't question him any further about his background. She assumed there must have been a reason he didn't want to talk about it. "As far as I'm concerned," he once stated to her, "the past is history."

Besides his seemingly eccentric traits, their union was steamy and passionate. They'd think nothing of going skinny dipping in a lake, and then he'd make passionate love to her somewhere seclude

CHAPTER THREE

Brandon's chief enjoyment was sailing, and he owned a sailboat. He couldn't wait to take Jenna sailing with him. He looked forward to taking the boat out on weekends, leisurely coasting on a lake somewhere, and over the summer months they sailed on a couple of different lakes, such as Pigeon Lake and Lake Clair in Alberta, which are between the East Lake and the Athabasca Lake. Lake Clair was more remote than the other two, and he enjoyed the tranquility of it.

After five months of dating and while cruising one Saturday afternoon on Lake Clair, Brandon asked Jenna to marry him. "My sweet Jenna, would you marry me?"

Excited, she jumped up and hugged him. "I thought you'd never ask." She was ecstatic. "Yes, I will marry you."

He pulled her close to him as he gently stroked her face with his fingers. Sliding his hands down the side of her slim body, he gently stroked her right breast. Looking with intensity into her eyes, he said, "I wanted to get to know you better, and now that I have, the time feels right for me to ask you for your hand in marriage."

His gentle but firm touch made her tremble inside, which she had never experienced with other men.

They decided to hold the wedding ceremony at a church in Tuscany, Italy. They couldn't ask for a better wedding day. It was a gorgeous bright clear day, with the sun's golden rays beaming over a calm Adriatic Sea.

Jenna wore a simple A-line satin wedding gown with just a few beads decorating a scooped neckline, and a tiara made from fresh flowers crowned her head. Brandon looked particularly suave in his white tuxedo style suit. Together they made an attractive looking couple.

Jenna had asked her best friend Andrea to be her matron-of-honor. She looked lovely in her soft green satin gown and matching bouquet of flowers. Andrea was happy for Jenna.

She had finally found someone who seemed to truly care for her.

The ceremony was beautifully orchestrated. Vases filled with white flowers and white candles lined the aisles, and at the end of each pew hung white satin ribbons.

The procession began with an Italian love song, then as the ceremony continued, soft classical music played in the background. The whole affair was like a fairy tale come true for Jenna.

After the ritual, they celebrated with friends and relatives down by the sea, but no one from Brandon's side of the family attended their wedding. She wondered why, and she asked him. He just said that it was too complicated to explain and he didn't offer any other explanation. She didn't pressure him for one.

For their honeymoon, they continued to travel to different Italian cities, enjoying magnificent sceneries and taking some time to bask in the sun on one of the white sandy beaches. They were lying on a blanket when he pointed up to the sky. "What is that up in the sky?"

Jenna glanced up, unconcerned. "I don't know. There are so many different things nowadays, you can't keep up with what's up there."

"It's definitely not a plane. It looks like a black mass . . . and look at those weird stringy formations around it. It's fascinating, isn't it?" It was as if he was trying to make her see something there that was more than just a black mass. She was baffled by his remark.

It hovered over them for a time, then vanished. Not bothering to look and not fully recognizing the similarities that had surrounded Gary's death, she said, "Oh! Who cares? Whatever it is, it's not bothering anyone. Let's just enjoy this fantastic scenery."

Agitated by her lack of interest, he said, "I know it doesn't matter to you."

"There are a lot of odd things in this world, Brandon. Why are you worried about a black mass?" Jenna asked.

"I'm not worried. You just don't understand."

"What is there to understand? Explain it to me?" Jenna asked, feeling somewhat irritated.

Brandon stood up and mumbled something under his breath. "Ah! Just forget about it, OK. Come on, let's go somewhere else." He grabbed her by the hand and off they went to see more sights.

Time flew by as they took in the great sites, dined at fabulous Italian restaurants, and enjoyed the wonderful Italian artifacts and museums. Soon, it was time for Brandon and Jenna to head back to Alberta.

After their honeymoon was over, they settled into an apartment in Alberta, but not for long. They wanted to live somewhere warmer and decided to purchase a home in Las Cabos, Mexico. After searching for a few months, they found a stunning home.

Jenna took great pleasure in decorating their new house with antique furnishings and accessories to match. She took delight in decorating the outside as well: the landscaping design was astonishing, the way she used an assortment of pink, bright purple, and yellow flowers with complimentary shades of greenery. A glittering kidney shaped swimming pool with a cabana for visitors filled the entire backyard, adding an extra feature to their charming home.

They planned to have guests over for barbecues. Brandon bought a stainless-steel barbeque and had a glassed-in wine rack built in. Their home contained everything they could ever hope for.

The economics department for a large financial firm in Las Cabos hired Brandon to be a supervisor, as far as Jenna knew, and he seemed to be excited about his new position.

Jenna, on the other hand, wanted to do something entirely different, and she chose to be involved in the tourist industry as a tour guide. It was a good position for her to meet new people and develop other friendships.

It was an exhilarating time for both. They received invitations to social gatherings, where they met lots of new and influential people like the CEO of Brandon's company and mayor of Las Cabos, who would benefit them in stabilizing their new careers by introducing them to different prospects, especially for Jenna as a tourist guide. They were settled and happy with their surroundings.

On a bright, hot Sunday morning in July, Brandon and Jenna set out on his sailboat. As an experienced seaman, Brandon felt confident navigating on Lake Clair. He inspected the backstay to make sure the tension was correct, tightened the rigging, and checked for anything that might present a problem. Although Jenna didn't know how to steer a sailboat, she liked being on the water. It felt to her like being in heaven.

There wasn't a cloud to be seen in the bright blue sky. The water was calm and clear with barely a wave lashing against the bow. The sails were the only thing that moved, shaking ever so slightly as the clipper bent on its side. Other than a slight bending, the boat glided smoothly down the lake as if it knew the direction. They looked forward to a great day just coasting along.

They thought to sail for a while, then anchor somewhere further down the lake and go for a swim. Brandon was a strong swimmer, and Jenna enjoyed swimming just as much he did. They were a good match athletically. It became a game with them, testing each other to see how fast and how far out they could go.

Jenna had a lithe body and strong legs, and she kept herself in good physical shape. She wasn't the type of person that liked fussing with her hair, and before they set sail, she cut her shoulder-length hair into a bob, which suited her auburn-coloured tresses perfectly. This hairstyle would be easier for her to manage after swimming.

Brandon's salt and pepper hair always became unruly after being in the water, but Jenna didn't mind his disorderly appearance, running her hand through his unmanageable strands.

"Is this what you do to all men's hair?" he grinned. He was not used to having women fuss over him in such a manner.

She smiled. "Not usually. I just like playing around with your hair. . ."

"You do amusing things sometimes, Jenna."

She looked at him, again puzzled by his remark, but she also realized that his personality was different in some respects from most of the men she knew.

Following their rigorous exercise, they sat on the deck chairs to enjoy the summer's gentle breeze against their faces, and they had a glass of wine and a snack. Jenna had brought a splendid Italian vintage red wine, which she purchased on their honeymoon while travelling through Italy. They both liked its fruity-smooth texture. She had also filled a picnic basket with a few snacks for something to munch on.

As they drifted along, Brandon picked up his binoculars to look out toward the centre of the lake.

"What are you looking at?" Jenna asked.

With an expression of apprehension on his face he said, "I'm not sure. There's something odd coming this way."

"What do you mean? Besides another boat, a whale or some other creature, what else could there be?"

"It's not a boat. It's a weird looking black fog, like the last one we saw in Italy, remember? Only it's bigger this time."

Jenna felt a sudden alarm, but pretended it didn't matter to her. "No, I can't say I do remember." Even though it bothered her, she didn't express her feelings and decided to have a look to appease him.

"Can I have a peek?" She grabbed the binoculars from his hand and looked through them. She saw nothing. "I don't see anything, Brandon. Maybe your eyes are playing tricks on you?"

"What do you mean you don't see anything?" He said gruffly as he reached for the binoculars. "Hand them back to me, there is something there. I can't believe you're not seeing it."

"OK, let me have another look." She looked again, and still she saw nothing. She didn't know what else to say and said, "Sorry, my eyes must be out of focus today."

"You must have a problem, because it's clearly there."

She thought it best to let it go. Whatever it was, it wasn't important enough to argue with him about.

He stood scanning at starboard a few moments. He didn't speak at first. Then he yelled, "Come here! It's coming closer."

In sheer exasperation, she walked over to him and grabbed the binoculars to have another look, and again she saw nothing.

"Brandon, I don't know what you're seeing. Maybe your mind is forming things for some reason. I really don't see anything, Brandon, honest."

"Oh, come on, do you think I'd make this up? You're frustrating me. Why don't you go below for a while?"

She stared at him, worried, wondering what was going on with him. She had never seen him so irritated before. Following his suggestion, she went below to lay down and nap for a half-hour. *Surely, he'll feel better in a while*, she thought.

She started dozing off when she heard a strange noise above, but she couldn't quite make it out; it didn't sound like footsteps.

She quietly climbed up the ladder then stood at the top looking out. Brandon wasn't where she thought he'd be, and she could no longer hear the sound.

Stepping further onto the deck, she called out, "Brandon, where are you? What was that noise I heard a few minutes ago?" There was only silence in response. She wondered where he could have gone. It was a fair-sized boat, but it wasn't by any means massive!

Jenna was flustered and skirted around the clipper. Much to her dismay, there was no sign of Brandon. She looked over the side, thinking maybe he went for a swim.

"Brandon, if you're playing a game with me, it isn't funny," she hollered. After scanning the water for a few moments and not seeing him, she fetched her cell phone from below and returned to the deck to make a call, but it wasn't picking up any signals. Frightened, she said, "I can't believe this! Of all times for this phone not to work."

Not knowing what else to do, she remembered there were flares on board and decided that she should light a flare. Before lighting it, she gazed out toward the lake, thinking perhaps there was something she had missed. All she could see was a big empty lake; nothing floated or moved about. "He must have fallen overboard and is hanging on for his life!" she cried.

Walking around once more, she checked the starboard and the back for anything that might give her a clue to Brandon's disappearance. Finding nothing, she went below again, conjecturing maybe he snuck by her, somehow. It was futile—he wasn't there either. She then ran toward the head. It was then that she spotted a piece of his shirt hanging onto the sideboard, and dribbling down the side was a gooey white substance. She resisted touching the dreadful looking stuff.

"Oh, my God! He has fallen overboard!" she screamed. Tears rolled down her cheeks, and losing hope, she collapsed on the deck floor. "What will I do now?"

Something made her look forward. Not far from the boat, she noticed a black mass just like the one Brandon had described. Jenna wondered why she hadn't noticed it before. It hovered over the boat for a few minutes, then quickly disappeared.

She was distraught and needed to get back to land. She attempted to manoeuvre the boat, but she wasn't strong enough to handle it.

Suddenly, the mass reappeared. "What is that thing?" she yelled out loud. It hung over the top of the boat for a short time and then disappeared again. She was frantic trying to figure out what was going on. It was all so unbelievably mystifying.

She started to light the flare when something dropped from the sky onto the deck. Rushing to pick it up, Jenna was surprised to see it was Brandon's medal—he was never without it. He told her that he had received it as a token for his bravery while in the military. All the old emotions she'd had about Gary's death came flashing back, and she bellowed, "I don't understand. What is this supposed to mean? Lord, please help me!"

In her despair, she lit the flare and sat down on a chair, waiting, unsure of what was going to happen next.

The day had nearly gone by when finally, toward dusk she saw a ship approaching. A man waved from starboard. Relieved that someone had seen the flare and came to her rescue, she frantically waved back, sobbing.

Jenna was safely taken back to her home. After a few days, the police contacted her, saying they did a thorough investigation of the sailboat in and out. Scuba divers searched for days. Brandon's body was never found.

CHAPTER FOUR

For quite some time after the strange incidents with Gary and then Brandon, Jenna locked herself up in her apartment. All she did was watch television and eat takeout meals.

Jenna was emotionally distraught and felt unable to be around people. She cried until her eyes stung. She prayed, asking, *what is wrong with me that these things are happening?*

Andrea tried calling her several times, but Jenna never returned her calls.

She decided to go directly to Jenna's apartment. Pounding on the door, she hollered, "Jenna, I know you're in there. This has gone on long enough."

Jenna didn't utter a word.

Andrea banged harder. "I'll keep banging on this door until you open up!"

"Leave me alone. I'm not in the mood," Jenna replied.

"I'm not leaving. If I have too I'll get someone to break this door down. Which do you prefer?" Andrea strongly said.

There was no response for several minutes. Finally, she heard the door latch unlock. Jenna slowly opened the door. She looked dreadful. She hadn't washed her hair in days. Her eyes were almost swollen shut from crying, and she was basically skin and bones.

Andrea let herself in. "Oh, my God, Jenna! You look terrible. You need to get out of here. Keeping yourself locked up this way is not a solution. I know you have been through hell in the past few years, but you need to move on with your life. You did all that you could under the circumstances. If the authorities couldn't help you, then who else could have? Let it go once and for all."

Jenna looked at Andrea, grief-stricken. She felt like a zombie. Too much had happened, and she had too many unanswered questions. She couldn't sleep or think clearly.

Andrea grabbed Jenna by the shoulders, shaking her.

"Jenna, get it together. You must get help. This has gone on long enough. It's time for you to get professional help."

"You don't know how I feel. You have never been through what I have. How can you be so blasé about everything?"

"I know I haven't been through what you have, but I care about you. It concerns me to see you this way. Take a good look in the mirror; you can't go on this way. None of us know the real reason why certain things occur in life. There may be an explanation, and you may never know it. You can't stay in this condition forever. It won't solve those mysteries or serve you in a positive way."

"I know you care. But everything in my life has no meaning for me anymore. Nothing is making any sense," Jenna said, dropping her head down.

"It will feel like that until you get some help. Give yourself credit for surviving it all."

"I suppose . . . I should get help."

"Jenna, listen to me, you need to get help, now."

After Andrea's urging and with her support, Jenna sought professional counselling. Several months went by before she felt comfortable socializing again.

Her acquaintances and friends were really concerned about her state of mind. Her birthday was coming up, so a few of them decided to throw her a birthday party. They arranged a surprise party at one of her favourite restaurants.

Andrea suggested to Jenna that she go out for dinner with her. Although she was reluctant at first, after a few minutes of Andrea's prodding, she agreed to go.

As they walked into the restaurant, everyone there stood up and sang, "Happy Birthday Jenna."

Overwhelmed with emotion, Jenna broke down in tears. Every person who attended the party came up and hugged her. She never realized that so many people cared about her well-being. It turned out to be a great evening, and it made her feel much better.

Sometime after the party, and after so many telling her she needed to get on with things, Jenna decided to move on with her life. Her idea was to quit her present job and start fresh, moving somewhere entirely different and find a job doing something else.

CHAPTER FIVE

Jenna combed various newspapers for jobs outside the province, but nothing caught her immediate interest. Unsure, she dithered back and forth about moving away from what she had known all her life or staying put in Alberta.

While doing some shopping one afternoon, she picked up a fashion magazine. A large clothing firm in Paris, France was advertising for a clothing consultant. Although she didn't have experience in that field, she was a fast learner and had always wanted to travel to France. *This could be a great opportunity for me to start all over again, doing something entirely different,* she thought.

She wanted to speak to Andrea about this job posting and texted her, "Want to meet for lunch today? I'd like to discuss an important matter with you."

"Sure. How about Angelo's on Cedar Street, 12:30?"

"Great, see you there," Jenna texted back.

Andrea arrived early and waited for Jenna. At 12:30 PM sharp, Jenna walked into the restaurant.

"Hi, you're looking a bit better," Andrea said.

"Thanks. I'm feeling better," Jenna replied.

"So, what's up?

Jenna's face showed excitement and she eagerly sat down. "I was looking for a position in some of the different newspapers from outside of the province when I found this ad in a magazine advertising for a clothing consultant in France." Jenna handed Andrea the ad she'd cut out, and with an excited tone she said, "It sounds really interesting. I'm thinking it could be a great opportunity for me to start a brand-new chapter in my life. What do you think?"

"France! Are you sure you would like living there? You don't know anyone and you don't speak fluent French, let alone know how to be a clothing consultant!"

"I can learn. France is a lovely country with lots of things to do, great places to see, and I will meet new people."

Unsure about Jenna's decision, Andrea said "Mm, I don't know, Jenna. But if you really think you would be happy living there, then go for it."

Disappointed at Andrea's lack of enthusiasm, Jenna picked up a napkin. Placing it on her lap, she said, "You don't seem very excited for me."

"It's not that I'm not excited for you. I'm just concerned about you being comfortable living there, not knowing anyone."

"That's the whole point! It would be a whole new beginning for me, and maybe that's what I need to do. Perhaps there's a reason I saw this ad, and this is telling me I should pursue it."

"Let's order. Then we'll continue talking about this idea of yours. I think I'm going to have the Chicken Primavera with a Mediterranean salad. That sounds scrumptious. What are you going to have?" Andrea asked Jenna.

"My appetite is still not what it should be. The Caesar salad will be fine."

Andrea continued to make her point about living in France. "It's an expensive place to live, and it would mean that you would have to make a lot more money to manage your expenses while living in Paris, and you don't know anything about the fashion industry."

"I'm aware how high priced things are in Paris, but I want to give it a shot. I won't worry about that, and I'm a fast learner. I can be persuasive when I want to be. What do I have to lose but time and money? Who knows what it could bring about in my life?" Jenna gestured with her hands trying to make her point stronger.

Andrea sat back for a moment before continuing. "If that's what you really want to do, Jenna, maybe it's what you need to do now in your life."

Jenna was quiet for a few moments, thinking about living in Paris, France.

The two women finished their meals, and each had a glass of wine to celebrate Jenna's new adventure. As they sat sipping on their wine, Andrea noticed a man standing at the end of the bar. He stared at them with a rigid gaze, making her feel creeped out. An eerie chill rolled up and down her spine.

"Jenna, do you know who that man is, standing over there? He's glaring at us. Something about him troubles me."

Feeling alarmed, Jenna turned and looked toward where the man stood. "No, I have no idea who he is."

He was of medium height and dressed in a black one-piece outfit, like a uniform. There was a menacing hardness about his eyes and a prominent scar across his right cheek made him even more unapproachable.

"I think we should leave. I'm feeling very uncomfortable with the way he's eyeing us. He's giving me the heebie-jeebies," Andrea said.

"You're right. Let's go."

They paid the bill and were quick to leave. As Jenna got into the car, she noticed the same man standing in the doorway of the restaurant. His eyes had a red glow about them as he watched them drive away.

"He's freaking me out." Jenna felt her heart heating fast, and her forehead was beading with sweat. Pressing her foot hard to the pedal, she quickly drove away.

CHAPTER SIX

By the end of September, Jenna was packed and ready to leave for Paris. She gathered all the household goods that she and Brandon had accumulated while they were they were married and donated them to a goodwill organization, and she left her car with Andrea.

She hadn't continued to live in the home that she and Brandon owned in Las Cabos, moving back to Alberta soon after his disappearance. She decided it was best to sell. There were too many memories associated with the house, and felt it necessary for her to get rid of everything that reminded her of the past.

On the day of her departure, the sky was a deep turquoise blue, and it was a beautiful sunny day. She watched the birds as they prepared to fly south. She loved watching them as they flew in a synchronized formation.

Jenna felt excited, but at the same time apprehensive. Living in Paris would be very different.

Although she had travelled by plane to other places, this flight seemed to be the longest she had ever taken. Luckily it was a smooth trip and she was glad.

Jenna sat back and opened the magazine she had bought before boarding the plane. There was an article about a company expanding its designing business. She thought, *this must be an omen that I'm doing the right thing. It's the second time I have seen a similar article*, and she sat back to relax, thinking about her new adventure. It wasn't long before she nodded off.

Jenna jerked up when the pilot announced their descent. The jitters she felt were pervasive. *Calm down, calm down*, she thought.

As she made her way toward the baggage collection area, she noticed a man by the baggage depot gawking at her, like the way the man in Angelo's restaurant did. His eyes, just as the other creepy man's, unveiled a stony glare, and he was dressed in the same fashion. He was younger than the other man from the restaurant. *Am I getting paranoid, or are these men following me?* she wondered.

Even though Jenna tried to shake off the unwanted trepidation she felt, the idea that these two men were following her hung at the back of her mind like a predator, making it necessary for her to get as far away from this individual as possible. She picked up her luggage and hurried to hail a taxi. Before getting in the cab, she glanced around to see if she could still see him, but she didn't. She told the driver to drive as fast as possible to the hotel where she had booked a room for the night.

The moment she checked in to her hotel, she called Andrea. "Hi, it's Jenna."

"How was your flight?" Andrea asked.

Her voice quivered as she spoke. "The . . . flight was fine, but when I picked up my bags, I saw another man glaring at me. He was dressed in the same way as that man at Angelo's. I don't know what to make of it. Why am I being followed? I'm scared, Andrea."

"Maybe it's just your imagination running wild right now, with everything changing so quickly. Take a deep breath and settle down. You've been through a lot. I think you're overreacting."

"I'll go soak in the bathtub for a while. Maybe that will help to calm my nerves."

"Good idea. Call me tomorrow. You will feel better by then. Have a good night's rest." Andrea hung up the phone feeling concerned about Jenna being alone in Paris.

Jenna immediately ran the water for a bath. She needed to relax and get her mind off things for a while. She poured a glass of wine and slipped into the bathtub, placed her wine on the ledge around the tub, and sat back to soak for a while.

CHAPTER SEVEN

The warmth of the hotel room gave Jenna some comfort. It was beautifully furnished with a comfy sofa and a matching floral-patterned chair. A thick comforter covered the bed, and a welcome gift sat on the table: a plate filled with hors d'oeuvres and different snacks. She was starved and devoured a few pieces.

Before falling asleep that night, she pulled open the drapes to allow the sunshine to seep through the window in the morning. She was up far enough that no one could see in.

The next morning as Jenna awakened, the sun's bright rays shone through the room like thin golden gossamers. It was a great way to start the day.

While doing, a few stretching exercises, she decided to begin her first day in Paris with a hearty breakfast, then take a stroll around the city streets to get a feel for her new surroundings.

The atmosphere in Paris was not at all like that of Prince George, Alberta, where she was from. The hustling and bustling of the city life seemed entirely different. There was a constant beeping of horns, people yelled out their windows in French, and there were many hand gestures being made. Women and men flaunted about in their fashionable attire as though expected.

There were a few cafés in the nearby vicinity that provided great breakfasts. She crossed the busy street to a quaint little café. As she walked in, she noticed French music played in the background.

A waitress came up to her table. "Bonjour, Madame. Quest-que vous desirer?"

"I'm sorry, I don't speak French. Is there someone here who speaks English?"

"Oui! Une moment sil-vous plait." The waitress walked off to get a waiter who spoke English.

As Jenna waited, she thought to herself, *I'll will need to get a command of the language soon, if I'm to live here.*

A tall, slim man sauntered up to her table. "Good day to you, Mademoiselle. My name is Robert. How can I help you today?"

"I would like to see the breakfast menu, please."

"Certainly, Mademoiselle."

He stepped into a room at the back of the café. She could hear him making a rude comment to a waitress. "These snobby English, why don't they learn how to speak our language before they decide to come Paris." He knew how to speak English, but he was determined not to unless he absolutely had to.

Jenna felt embarrassed. She knew her lack of French language skills was going to be a problem in the beginning. The waiter came back and handed her the menu, explaining to her what breakfasts were available. He seemed agitated, but he at least tried to be pleasant.

She ordered a poached egg on a muffin, pan-fried taters, juice, and a cup of French coffee.

"Will that be all, Mademoiselle?"

"Oui, merci beaucoup," she said, trying to make an effort to speak French. Even though the waiter's facial expression appeared unsympathetic, he placed the order.

After eating the delicious breakfast, Jenna sat back to enjoy a caramel coffee. The flavoured coffee tasted different from what she was used to; nonetheless, it was quite tasty. While she was enjoying her coffee, for a split second, she thought she noticed the same man that was at the airport sitting at the back of the café. "This is ridiculous, what my mind can do to me, sometimes!" she exclaimed. She tended to over imagine things at times, and she thought it was her overzealous imagination.

Jenna didn't have any definite plans right away, so she decided to take in some of the sights and hired a cab driver for the day. He drove through Paris's busiest locations. The city felt magical. She was amazed by its activities. There were a lot things to see and do—she didn't know where to start.

She asked the cab driver where she should go first. "Can you suggest some places?"

"Oh! Mons Dieux, Mademoiselle, so many tings. De Eiffel Tower is a good place. Den dere is de tour of the Versailles Gardens and Palace and de Louvre. Dat might be enough for you today, Mademoiselle. It is a lot to see all at once; dis is up to you."

"Please, take me to the Louvre first."

The Louvre was phenomenal with its ancient exhibitions and painting. It was by far one of the best museums she had ever seen. She read the historical excerpts about the museum:

*The building has been extended many times over time to form the present Louvre Palace. In 1682, Louise XIV chose the Palace of Versailles for his household, leaving the Louvre primarily as a place to display the royal collections. From 1692, there was a collection of ancient Greek and Roman sculptures, and the collection is divided among eight curatorial departments: Egyptian Antiquities; Near Eastern Antiquities; Greek, Etruscan, and Roman Antiquities; Islamic Art; Sculpture; Decorative Arts; Paintings; Prints and Drawings.

The museum opened on August 10th, 1793, with an exhibition of 537 paintings, many of the works being royal and confiscated church property. Because of structural problems with the building, the museum was closed in 1796 for a period. The collection then increased under Napoleon, and the museum was renamed the Musée Napoleon, but after his abdication, many works were seized by his armies and were returned to their original owners. The collection further increased during the reigns of Louis XVIII and Charles X, and during the Second French Empire, the museum gained 20,000 pieces.[*]

She found the historical tour incredible. Awestruck, she strolled through the many corridors looking at the varied artifacts.

The day flew by, and before she realized it, it was time to get back to her hotel room. She paid the driver and stepped

---

[*] Information about the Louvre and its ancient artifacts and history found in the Wikipedia Encyclopedia.

into her hotel lobby, looking forward to having a light dinner then soaking in the tub for a while again.

As she proceeded toward the elevator, she noticed the same strange man that she thought she saw at the café standing by a large ornamental tree in the lobby. *Enough is enough, I've got to find out why he's following me.* At full tilt, she walked toward him. But before she could reach him, he vanished. *This is getting stranger by the hour,* she thought.

Feeling angst-ridden about this whole affair she approached the clerk. "Hello, my name is Jenna Paxton. I have a room up on the sixth floor. Did you by chance notice a man standing over by that ornamental tree? I think he's following me."

"Non, Mademoiselle, I did not see him. If you are concerned about this person, do you want me to call the police?"

"Not now, but if I see him again, then I will have you call them."

"C'est biens, if you are certain."

"Yes, thank you. I will let you know."

"Bons soit, Mademoiselle."

"Bons soit." Without hesitation, Jenna hurried to get to her room.

She braced herself as she walked out of the elevator, checking the hallway before going into her room. She didn't see any sign of the mysterious character, but she quickly entered the room and locked the door.

CHAPTER EIGHT

The next morning, after enjoying a croissant with bacon and eggs and a café aux lait at a café, Jenna made her mind up to return to the museum to see more of the antiquities. Today she wanted to concentrate on the Egyptian art and the history behind it. She was fascinated by those art pieces. The departments within the museum were expansive, taking more time for her to walk around and see all the different works of art, especially the Egyptian section.

Jenna was meandering about the Egyptian artifacts when suddenly, an envelope and a button fell to the ground in front of her. She looked up to see where they fell from, but there was nothing up there except the ceiling. She picked up the button and the envelope. She trembled. *This is weird, it looks like a button from Gary's favourite shirt.* There was a tiny insignia on it: a small circle within a larger circle and a half-moon. She didn't understand the meaning behind the symbols or even if they meant anything at all. She opened the envelope and read the note inside. *"Soon, you will know the truth."* Jenna felt sick to her stomach and wondered what it was all supposed to mean. Even though she felt unsettled, she put the strange items in her coat pocket and finished the tour, but she couldn't really concentrate on it any longer. She needed to go get back to her hotel room. Though she would have liked to have seen more, she felt an urgent need to call Andrea.

Jenna's mind raced feverishly, wondering about who it was that followed her, and now the button and the message that had appeared—what was the meaning behind them? The whole situation was getting more and more peculiar. She was convinced that two men followed her; the question was, why?

The cab driver dropped her off in front of the hotel. Getting out of the cab, she quickly glanced around to see if anyone watched her, and straightaway she went to her room. She flung her shawl onto a chair and immediately dialed

Andrea's number. It rang and rang. She got Andrea's voice answering service and left a message. "Hi, Andrea, it's me," she said anxiously. "I need to talk to you as soon as you get home. It's very important. Please call me back."

She hung up. Still anxious and not knowing what else she should do, she called the Paris police.

"La agent de police, André. Comment je pourais vous aidee?"

"Agent André. I'm sorry, but I don't speak French. I need to speak to someone who speaks English."

"I speak English. How can I help you?"

"Would you or another police officer be able to come to the hotel where I am staying? There is something important I need to report. I have just moved here to Paris from Canada, and I believe there are two men following me."

"Are you sure you are being followed, Madame?" the officer asked.

"Yes, I'm quite sure," Jenna replied.

"What hotel and room number?"

"Paris France Hotel, room 636 on the sixth floor."

"An officer will be there within the hour, Mademoiselle."

"Thank you, Agent André." She hung up feeling puzzled and disturbed by the recent occurrences. Her hand shook as she poured herself a glass of wine. Fear was starting to overwhelm her. Unable to keep still, she paced around the room, thinking about what was going on. What had she done to invite these strange incidences into her life?

The buzzer rang, and Jenna quickly answered it. "This is Agent André from the downtown precinct. You asked for a police officer?"

"Yes, please come up." She felt shaky inside as she waited for him.

In a few minutes, she heard a knock. She opened the door to let him in.

"Please come in and have a seat. My name is Jenna Paxton," she said showing him the sofa.

"Now, Miss, what is your concern?" he asked her as he stepped inside the doorway.

"I just moved to Paris from Alberta, Canada. I've had some very mysterious events going on in my life for the last few years, and now it seems there are two men following me here in Paris, and it's frightening me."

"Please, give me the details." Agent André was intrigued, and he bent forward further to pay greater attention to what she was about to tell him.

Jenna told him everything about her experiences, first with Gary, and then with Brandon and what had happened to her so far since coming to Paris.

"Those circumstances are very strange, Miss, but what gives you the impression these men are following you here? Were these two men Caucasian, black, or from some other ethnic background?" he asked.

"I have seen them watching me a few times. I'm sure they are following me. I didn't get a good look at them, but I think they were both Caucasian. One was younger than the other. And then this button and envelope fell in front of me in the lobby of the Louvre."

With a serious expression on her face, she showed him the button and the envelope with the message. "I have no idea where they came from or what they mean. There was nothing except the ceiling above me." She paused. "The button looks like the same type that was on one of Gary's favourite shirts. It's not your usual run of the mill shirt button," she said, handing it to him with trembling hands.

He took the button out of her hand and looked at it for a couple of minutes and then read the note. His immediate thought was that maybe Jenna was on drugs and delusional.

"Interesting," he said, not really knowing what to make of it. "The button does have an odd emblem on it. I have seen different symbols like this, but not exactly like this one. There could be another reason why this button was on the ground, though. It may have fallen from someone else's shirt. As far as the note, it could be just be a coincidence. It's obvious you're upset, but this is not a lot to go on, Ms. Paxton. How do you know for certain that this note was meant for you? Unless there is an actual threat being made on your life, I cannot help you."

"You mean to say, unless someone kills me, you won't consider this matter?" Jenna said, taken aback. "Wow! That's not very encouraging. I'm certain I'm being followed, agent André. I saw the one man a couple of times. And both men wore the same black one-piece suit. Not only that, but when they stared directly at me, their eyes had a strange red glow about them. Tell me," she said, getting angry, "does that seem normal to you?"

Rolling his eyes, he replied, "Ms. Paxton, at the present time, there have been no life-threatening attempts. I cannot do anything until such a time that there is an actual threat. Keep a close vigilance. If there is a threat made upon your life, then I will certainly look deeper into the matter. Here is my card with my direct number. In the meantime, may I suggest that it might be a good idea to have someone stay with you?"

"I don't know anyone here," Andrea said, taking the card and looking down at it. "It's really upsetting to know that unless my life is in danger, and you will not help."

She stood up from the sofa and paced around the room. A glum expression on her face indicated her mental unrest. "Is this a policy of all police departments in France?" she curtly asked.

"I can only say that it is a standard procedure in our department. We cannot be expected to follow up on these types of calls. We need more evidence than what you have here," he replied, trying not upset her any more than she was already.

"I'm terribly disappointed. I was hoping to make a fresh start in Paris. How am I going to go about my life here, feeling threatened this way?"

Agent André fidgeted, agitated by Jenna's pacing. "I repeat," he said slowly, "unless there is an actual attempt made on your life, there is nothing I can do for you. Why not contact someone you know back home and ask them if they could come to stay with you for a while?"

"I don't know if it would be possible for anyone back in Canada to come here right now," she said, feeling very uneasy.

The agent stood up, getting ready to leave. "I apologize that I couldn't be more helpful. Ms. Paxton. Be attentive to your surroundings. If there is a threat made upon you, don't hesitate to call, or have someone else call me if you aren't able for whatever reason. Good night, Ms. Paxton."

As she watched the agent walk out of the room, Jenna felt like she was losing control. She desperately tried to figure out what was happening. *What am I supposed to do?* She wondered, again.

CHAPTER NINE

Jenna shuddered as she picked up the phone to dial Andrea's number. Andrea answered this time. "Hello."

"Andrea, it's me!" Jenna shrieked into the phone.

"Whoa! Easy does it. What's the matter?"

"I'm positive there are two men following me. I called the police, but they can't help me unless my life is threatened," she said, panicked. Jenna continued to talk, telling Andrea about the envelope with the weird message and the button she found at the Louvre.

"An envelope with a strange message and a button! Geez, Jenna, I don't know what to say about that. I can't help you, being so far away."

"Would you consider coming here to stay with me for a little while?" Jenna asked, with panic in her voice.

"I don't have any vacation time left. I'm not sure if I can arrange any more time," Andrea replied hesitantly.

"I'm scared, Andrea. I need you here."

"It's obvious by the tone of your voice that you're afraid. I'll see what I can do." Andrea paused before saying anything else. "I'll call you back as soon as I find out if I can get some vacation time. In the meantime, talk to the desk clerk. Maybe he or she can suggest something that can help you. I am so sorry this is happening to you." Andrea didn't know if she could help her friend, but she felt bad for her.

"Thanks, Andrea. I would really appreciate it if you could come out here for a while. Let me know. I probably won't sleep much tonight."

"Try. You have to rest to keep your strength up."

"I know. That's easier said than done."

"I will be thinking of you. Love you." Andrea hung up.

"Love you, too," Jenna said, and throwing the phone down, she fell sobbing onto the bed.

The next morning, Jenna woke up feeling terrible. Everything ached. She decided to stay in for the day to rest. She didn't have much of an appetite but wanted order in a light breakfast. She also wanted to have a shower, hoping it would make her feel better. Just as she was climbing into the shower, the phone rang. She rushed to pick it up.

"Hello? Hello?" Jenna said. She could hear raspy breathing, but no one at the other end spoke. She hung up and called the desk clerk. "This is Jenna Paxton in room 636. Did you call me just now?"

"Non, Mademoiselle, I did not. Is there a problem?"

"I'm not sure. Someone called here just in the last few minutes. I heard heavy breathing on the other end, but no one said anything."

"It was probably a wrong number," the clerk replied.

"Perhaps you're right. Could you pass me over to room service please? Thank you."

"One moment." The clerk transferred the call to room service.

"This is Jenna Paxton in room 636. I would like to have breakfast sent up to my room. I would like toast with jam, coffee, and a banana, if you have any."

"Not a problem, Madame. It will be about fifteen to twenty minutes."

"Thank you."

She shivered as she hung up and sat down on the sofa. "What in hell is going on? I won't be able to manage, if this keeps up!" she exclaimed out loud to an empty room.

The phone rang again. Jenna hesitated to answer, but then she thought that maybe it was Andrea calling.

Picking up the phone, she quietly said, "Hello . . ."

"Hi, it's Andrea. You don't sound so great. Is there more stuff going on since I last spoke to you?"

"I was afraid to answer the phone. I just got a strange call. I could hear heavy breathing on the line, but no one said anything. I called the desk clerk to see if they called me, but they said no."

"It must have been a wrong number," Andrea replied.

"That's what the clerk said, too. With everything that has gone on, every little thing is starting to get to me."

"There are certainly some strange things going on around you," Andrea commented. "I do have some good news. I could arrange a couple of weeks of holiday, although it means I won't be getting any more time off this year. My flight leaves tomorrow afternoon. I should be in Paris by evening."

"Oh, you're sweet!" Jenna said, relieved. "I love you for it. Call me as soon as you get here."

"I will. In the meantime, try and calm down. Have a couple of glasses of wine. That usually helps you to relax."

"I'm not going anywhere. I decided to stay in."

"Good idea. See you soon, Jenna. Take care."

CHAPTER TEN

Andrea arrived in Paris the following evening. She was worried about Jenna. So many weird things had gone on in her life. Andrea thought that it was all too much for Jenna to handle by herself. As soon as she got off the plane, she called her.

Jenna hadn't slept well again and had been up early that day. Waiting around made her feel even more anxious. She made herself a cup of coffee and ate a muffin while waiting for Andrea. It was about 5:00 PM. when the phone rang. Having been on edge, it startled her. Cautiously she answered, "Hello . . . who is it?"

"It's me Andrea. I just got in. I'm still at the airport. I should be at the hotel within the hour. Are you OK?"

"Yeah, so-so. I'm glad you're here. I didn't sleep very much last night. Why don't we go out for dinner as soon as you get here? I want to get my mind off things for a couple of hours, and having dinner out would be nice."

"Sure, but I would like to have a quick shower before we go out to eat. See you in a bit."

Jenna decided to have a shower to freshen up before Andrea arrived. When she looked in the mirror, she could see that dark circles were forming around her eyes. *Some makeup should help*, she thought.

The buzzer rang. "Is that you Andrea?" she asked as she answered.

"Be right up," Andrea replied.

Jenna stood by the door. Within a few minutes, there was a knock. She opened the door and let Andrea in.

"Hi," Andrea said as she walked into the room.

"I got here as fast as I could. How has everything been since we last spoke?"

"No more strange calls, thank goodness," Jenna replied with relief in her voice.

"I'll have a quick shower, and we'll talk about it over dinner." Andrea had a shower and slipped on some fresh clothes.

"OK, I'm ready," she said, coming out of the bathroom and feeling refreshed. "Get your coat on and let's go eat."

Jenna dragged herself to the closet to fetch her coat.

Andrea noticed the way she was dragging. "You look tired. How about after dinner we go to a spa for a massage? That might help to relax you. You may even fall asleep for a while."

"Yeah, that's sounds like a good idea," Jenna responded.

They walked to the closest restaurant. There was a fair-sized crowd inside, but it wasn't so busy or noisy that they couldn't have a conversation while they ate. Andrea checked her phone directory for spas. She found one not far from the restaurant, and they were open until 10:00 PM. She noticed there were quite a few conveniences close by the hotel, making it a perfect place to stay.

Both women ordered the chicken lasagna, and while eating, Andrea asked Jenna what she was planning to do about the men who were following her.

"I don't know what to do," Jenna responded, despairing. "Do I just carry on hoping nothing else will happen? Or do I try and find out why these men are following me?"

"What about hiring a detective? Have you considered that?"

"Detectives are not cheap," Jenna said.

"I can help you with some of the cost if you like. A detective may be able to find out who and why these men are following you."

"It's an avenue to consider. Let's check it out once we are done at the spa," Jenna responded.

They left the restaurant and walked further down the street where the spa was located. Andrea approached a woman standing at the counter. "Hello, could my friend and I book a massage, if possible?"

"Yes. We have had a cancellation and that appointment is available right now if that works for you and your friend."

Jenna smiled. She was glad they could get a massage right away.

All the massage remedies that the masseuse used worked to calm Jenna right down, and she fell asleep. The masseuse allowed Jenna to sleep a little longer after the massage was finished, because she could feel all the tension built up in Jenna's body.

Andrea sat and read while Jenna slept. An hour and a half later, Jenna finally woke up, feeling much better. She did a few stretches and some yoga poses to get her energy level back up.

"That was great, Andrea, thank you for suggesting it. I think I'm ready to go on with the rest of the evening."

"Alright, then let's check out detective agencies now," Andrea said. "Maybe with some luck on our side, we'll find one right away and get him or her started on investigating these stalkers. Why don't we ask the owner of the restaurant? He might know someone." They walked back to the restaurant to ask the owner if he knew of a good detective.

They spoke to the owner, and he did know a reputable detective named Detective Louis Chambeaux. His office was located just a few blocks from the hotel. They could walk up there in the morning.

However, the next morning, Jenna didn't feel up to walking the distance and they waved down a taxi.

As Jenna and Andrea approached the building where the detective's office was located, they saw a sign indicating that his office was on the third floor. They took the elevator up, and when they entered his office, Louis Chambeaux was busy looking at some documents

He stood up and greeted them. Jenna estimated him to be around six-feet-two. He was an attractive man with broad shoulders, a thin mustache, thick raven black hair, and dark, penetrating eyes. She thought to herself, *Mmm, a nice-looking man.*

"Detective Chambeaux," she said, as she extended her hand out, making herself appear as though she were more self-assured than she felt. "My name is Jenna Paxton, and this is my friend, Andrea Talbot. Do you speak English?"

"Yes, I do. How can I help you?"

"I'm the one that needs help. My friend, Andrea, is only staying with me for a few weeks."

"Please, sit down Miss Paxton, Miss Talbot, and tell me your concerns."

"Please, call me Jenna." Jenna said, still admiring the way he looked.

They sat down, and Jenna proceeded to tell Detective Chambeaux everything that had previously taken place with Gary and Brandon and what was now occurring in Paris.

CHAPTER ELEVEN

"It sounds to me as though you've experienced some very unusual incidents," Louis said after Jenna finished telling her story. "In regards to the two men who are following you, I can understand why you're fearful. For that situation, specifically, I would have to have someone do a stakeout to make sure the men don't harm you, and hopefully find out why they're following you. And you're questioning why your first husband died so suddenly, and why the second husband disappeared and was never found? It all sounds intriguing, that is without question. I would need to obtain more information to move forward with an investigation on those matters. I will need to know everything you know about these two men you were married to. What they did for a living, where they worked, any relatives, and so on."

"Aside from these details, would you be willing to take on this investigation based what on what I have told you so far about Gary and Brandon?" Jenna asked, feeling hopeful.

"I need more information about them before I begin," Louis replied.

"May I arrange for a time where we could sit down and I'll tell you everything I know about Gary and Brandon?"

"I have tomorrow morning at 10:00 available, if that is suitable."

"Yes, that would be fine." Jenna looked toward her friend. "I would like Andrea to be there as well."

"That is quite alright with me. Write down anything that you think might be a benefit to this investigation. I shall meet with both of you in the morning."

Jenna shook his hand. She realized she was staring at him. "Thank you Detective Chambeaux. I really need to know what's going on. I'm getting worn down with all that's happened lately."

"That's quite understandable. I shall see you both in the morning. Good day ladies," he said as he showed the women out.

As Andrea and Jenna left his office, they decided to purchase a bottle of wine. They were both tired and needed to get back to the hotel for some rest. There was a wine store not far from the hotel where they could get a variety of French wines. They wanted to try out a Parisian wine that evening.

They were walking to their hotel room after purchasing their wine, when Andrea noticed a man sitting on a lounge chair close to the elevator. As they got closer, he turned toward them and glared at them. She recognized him as the same man who was at the restaurant in Alberta.

The man wore a one-piece black outfit, and on his right cheek was a prominent scar. Jenna was preoccupied with digging in her purse for something and didn't see him sitting there, and Andrea didn't want to alarm her about his presence. Jenna would be extremely unnerved if she knew he was there. *I best not say anything to her just yet. She's been through enough*, Andrea thought. Andrea felt some anxiety of her own about the man being there at the hotel, though.

"Jenna, I need to get a couple of things at the variety store, go on up. I'll be there shortly," she said and motioned for Jenna to go.

"OK, get me a writing pad," Jenna said. "I want to jot down everything that comes to mind to give the detective tomorrow."

Andrea wanted to take a picture of the man with her cell phone. He was still sitting in the chair talking on a cell phone when she quietly sneaked up behind a large plant close to where he sat. She took a picture when he was looking straight ahead. She planned on showing it to the detective the next day.

She would mention it to Jenna in the morning before their meeting w

CHAPTER TWELVE

Jenna slipped on a pullover sweater and a pair of sweat pants, poured two glasses of wine, and waited for Andrea to return.

Andrea purchased a bottle of hand cream so that Jenna wouldn't wonder why she didn't get anything and picked up a writing pad for her.

Jenna felt anxious as she stood at the window looking out at all the bright lights of the city. Paris was a very busy city. People always seemed to be rushing around. Cars darted in and out of the traffic, seemingly without much concern about crashing into one another. She loved the city, but unless Louis had an answer for her, she felt that she might not be able to stay.

Andrea let herself in. "Did you get what you wanted?" Jenna asked.

"Yep, here's your writing pad."

"I'm going to write down everything that I can remember about Gary and Brandon and as much as I know about them personally. Maybe you can help, if there is something that I've forgotten or missed." A sudden gloom came over Jenna's face. "My nerves are shattered whenever I think about everything that happened in the past, but I know this needs to get done."

"Let's have wine while we make a list," Andrea suggested.

They spent the entire evening writing down what Jenna knew about the two men she had loved, and Andrea helped by jotting down some things she remembered about them.

The one aspect that stood out the most for Jenna was the fact that Brandon never wanted to speak about his past at all. At the time, when she was with him, she wondered why, but she never bothered to question it. Now, she realized, it may be something that would need to be considered for the investigation. Midnight rolled around by the time they finished making their notes, and it was time to get some sleep.

Jenna tossed and turned, getting up a few times during the night. Her mind refused to rest. At 7:00 AM. the next morning, she was ready and anxious to meet with the detective. Andrea slept in.

She couldn't wait any longer, "Andrea, wake up," she said, shaking her friend awake. "It's 8:00. We should have breakfast before we meet the detective."

Yawning and rubbing her eyes, Andrea said, "Holy moly! Jenna, you're up early. Take it easy will you. It will get done."

"I'm getting restless, just sitting around," Jenna said as she paced around the room.

"I know, but go easy on me, OK. I need my rest."

"Sorry."

Once Andrea was up, she had a quick shower and got dressed, feeling somewhat exasperated by Jenna's constant anxiety attacks.

They chose a different restaurant this time called Le Sixième Sens. It boasted of their strawberry French toast with natural maple syrup. Jenna's and Andrea's mouths salivated just thinking about the decadent food. It was a small place, but quaint, with an antique French style decor.

While they were eating their breakfasts, Andrea decided she should say something to Jenna about the man she saw in the lobby the night before.

"I have to tell you about something I saw yesterday. I didn't tell you at the time because I wanted you to get your mind off things for a night." Andrea paused, taking a sip of her coffee. "I saw that same man in the lobby yesterday, and I took a picture of him with my cell phone."

"What!" Jenna put her fork down and intently stared at Andrea. "And you didn't say anything to me? You know what, this must stop. I've got to find out why these men are following me, Andrea. I'm glad you took a picture. Maybe that will help the detective."

"I thought it best not to say anything right away. You're overwrought as it is. I hope it will help the detective."

"If you're finished, let's head over there now," Jenna said tersely. They flagged a taxi and asked the driver to take them to the detective's office.

As soon as the women entered the building, they saw Detective Chambeaux walking toward them. "Good morning ladies, please come in." He opened the door to let Jenna and Andrea inside. "I was just on my way to pick up a newspaper, but that can wait. You both seem a bit strained this morning. Has something else happened?"

"Yes, I am afraid so. Andrea saw the same man yesterday in the lobby of the hotel. She took a picture of him, thinking it might be of help," Jenna replied.

"Let me have a look at it."

The three of them walked into his office and Andrea passed her cell phone over to the detective. "I understand what you mean about the interesting outfit this man has on," Louis said as he looked at the picture. "I can see now why you're concerned, Jenna. He does appear menacing. I will transfer this picture onto my computer right now, so that I have it on hand. It may come in handy. Did you write everything down that you remembered about the two men you were married to?"

"Yes, and Andrea has also jotted down a few things that she remembered about them. There were a couple of things as I recall that seemed strange at the time, especially with Brandon. Should we just leave this information with you so that you can begin to consider this matter?" Jenna reached in her purse and pulled out the notepad, full of notes that she and Andrea had taken the night before.

"I have a few questions to ask you first. Please have a seat. My secretary made a fresh pot of coffee, would you like a cup?"

"Yes, please," Jenna answered.

"Just a half a cup for me, thanks," Andrea replied.

"Alright, then. I'll have Margaret bring t

CHAPTER THIRTEEN

Louis's office was tiny, and for all of them to sit around his desk, they had to squeeze in tightly. He continued to ask Jenna questions about Gary and Brandon. "What years did they die? Did they have any relatives or family? Where did they live before you knew them? Where did they work?"

Jenna answered the first question, the year Gary passed away and when Brandon disappeared, but she didn't know very much about Brandon's relatives—only small insignificant bits of information. Gary's parents lived in Vancouver as far as she was aware, but she had never met them. As for Brandon's parents, he never talked about them. However, she thought that they may have resided somewhere in California, based on a couple of comments Brandon had made.

"I'm sure you're aware that it will take me a bit of time to compile all this information, and I will need to make some phone calls to locate Gary's relatives," Louis told the women after he was done with the questions.

"I realize that," Jenna said. "The only problem is that Andrea must return home in a couple of weeks. She has to get back to work," she said, appearing anxious.

"Then I would suggest that you stay somewhere else other than the hotel. Perhaps the women's centre would be a safer place for you, especially when you are alone."

Jenna and Andrea looked at each other with a questioning expression. "You think it would be safer there?" Jenna asked.

"Yes," Louis said, adamantly. "They keep a close eye on things, and they will make sure that you are safe and comfortable."

"OK, we'll arrange it. I'll let you know when we are settled at the centre."

"Try not to worry. I will get started on this job right away, and hopefully I will have some answers for you within a couple of days."

"That would be wonderful," Jenna said, feeling hopeful. "I want to know why these men are following me, as well as more about what Gary and Brandon were involved in, of course."

"I'll get as much information about Gary and Brandon as I can, and I will follow through with finding out about these two fellows who are following you. I'll need to get someone to do a stakeout. As soon as I have anything that may provide some light on this situation of yours' I will get in touch with you."

"Thank you, Detective Chambeaux," Jenna said as she and Andrea stood up to leave. "We will be waiting to hear from you."

"Have a good day." Rubbing his chin as he walked back into his office, he wondered what kinds of interesting things this case would bring about.

Andrea and Jenna decided that they needed to decide to stay at the women's centre right away. Andrea pulled up the local directory on her phone. The place they were looking for was listed several blocks away from the hotel. That was fine with Jenna—being as far away from the hotel would be a good idea, and it would give her some peace of mind.

They wasted no time in gathering up their clothing and sundries. After making sure they had all their belongings, they hopped into a cab and went straight to the centre.

The women's centre was in a large building with barred windows. Jenna rang the buzzer, and a voice came over the intercom: "Bonjour, comment je pourais vous aidee."

"Bonjours, my name is Jenna Paxton and my friend is Andrea Talbot. Can you speak English?"

"Oui, un peux. Une moment sil vous plait." There was a brief pause and then someone with more fluent English spoke. "Good day ladies. What can I do for you?"

"My friend and I would like to stay at this centre for a couple of weeks." Jenna paused, considering. "Actually, it might be more than a couple of weeks, if that's possible?"

"Do you have any references?" the voice asked.

"Yes. Detective Louis Chambeaux recommended this place to us."

"Ah, yes! I know of Louis Chambeaux. I gather this is of a serious nature?"

"Yes, it is," Jenna replied.

The door was unlocked to let them in. An older woman with slicked back hair and wide eyeglasses greeted them once they were inside. She seemed to be examining them as she led them to an office.

"My name is Marianne, and I am the supervisor of the centre. Please sit down. Can you show me some identification?"

Jenna and Andrea both pulled out their birth certificates, health cards, which included a picture, and workplace references.

"Now then, tell me the reason for your stay here?" Marianne asked, as she examined their identification and references.

Jenna explained a little about what had occurred in Alberta and about the men who were following her back home and now Paris. She disclosed that Detective Chambeaux suggested they stay at the centre, because he thought it would be a safer place for them.

"It sounds like you're in need of a more secure place and that you might be in danger. However, we do have rules you will need to follow," she said with a stern look on her face. "If you need to go out for any length of time, we would appreciate being informed of your whereabouts and how long you plan on being away. We need to keep a record of everyone coming and going out of this centre. However, if there is a potential threat to your life or to the others staying here, we will immediately get the police involved. Do you understand?"

Both nodded. "Yes, we understand totally."

"Good. I shall take you to your room. If you require any toiletries or towels, please let the custodian know."

"Thank you very much. We appreciate you're taking us in," Jenna said.

"I trust that your situation will be resolved, soon. Dinner will be served at 6:00 in the dining area. Breakfast is usually around 7:00 AM. Lunch is not usually an option here, but we could provide you with a few things if you need to have lunch here." The woman gave Jenna the key and left them in front of the room that was to be theirs for a time.

Both walked into the room exhausted and fell on the bed. Neither spoke, but Jenna felt safer.

After a good while, Andrea said, "I'm going to have a shower before we eat. How about you?"

"Yes, I think I need a shower, too. I can hardly wait until all of this is behind me." Jenna sucked in some air quickly.

"Yeah, me too, for your sake."

Six o'clock rolled around, and it was time to have dinner. There were about a dozen women staying at the centre, ranging from middle teens to more mature in age. As Jenna and Andrea sat at the long dining table, the others welcomed them. Each one of them had a story to tell, and some were frightening.

A couple of the women asked Jenna and Andrea about their stories, but neither wanted to share too much information. Jenna said she was being harassed by her boyfriend and that Andrea was keeping her company for a time.

After dinner, Jenna and Andrea decided to go to bed early. It had been a long day.

CHAPTER FOURTEEN

Meanwhile, Louis began the investigation based on the information he had received from Jenna and Andrea. He immediately became fascinated by Brandon's character. From Jenna's description of him, especially the fact that he didn't want to discuss his past at all, he made for a captivating case. Louis wanted to make enquiries about him first, and then he would continue with investigating Gary. Instinctively, something told him there was a lot more to these two men than met the eye. His interest sharpened as he continued to read more, particularly about the events concerning the black masses.

Louis spent a whole day researching Brandon, trying to get information about his parents and places where he may have lived. He couldn't find anything at all about his parents or any other family. It was as if they never existed, which he found very puzzling. There were no records of any residences where Brandon had lived, except for the home he and Jenna shared together in Las Cabos, and supposedly he had lived in Alberta as well.   When he called the post office about the box number, he was told that it hadn't been used since it had first been applied for, which was now several years gone by.

What's with this bloke? he wondered, roughly scratching his forehead. The more he searched, the less information there was about Brandon. He couldn't find any banking activities for Brandon Styles in Alberta, or anywhere else for that matter. He supposedly worked for an economics company in Las Cabos, Mexico while he lived there with Jenna. Louis called the company and spoke to HR to inquire if Brandon had worked there in the past. They told him that no one with the last name of Styles was ever employed by them. That was extremely noteworthy to Louis.

All their financial transactions were apparently looked after in Jenna's name; none were done in his name. Maybe she wanted to oversee all their financial matters— he would need to ask her that question.

As he continued to make calls to Vancouver regarding any financial transactions Gary may have made, he hit another road block: he couldn't find anything about any financial transactions under the name of Thompson. He then checked for any type of information on Gary Thompson, but there didn't seem to be any records. The next day, he decided to concentrate more on all Thompson names instead, thinking maybe he would have better luck.

* * *

The following morning, Louis resumed his research. Although, he was starting to get frustrated, he was determined to get some answers that day. Finally, after a few hours of searching, he came across the information that Gary was employed by an environmental agency in Alberta for a short term. He planned on speaking with the company's supervisor or someone who was in charge.

Louis also found out that Gary did have relatives in Vancouver, who he planned to contact. Gary appeared to be slightly more transparent than Brandon, but aside from the one work record that he came across and a relative, nothing else seemed to indicate much about him, either.

Louis called Jenna to arrange a meeting with her to inform her of what information he had attained on Brandon and Gary so far.

Jenna answered, "Hello, who is speaking please?"

"Hi, Jenna. It's Louis Chambeaux. Can we get together this afternoon? I have some information to share with you."

"Sure. Let's meet at the café across from the centre around 12:30."

"OK, see you then."

Jenna hung up the phone, feeling uneasy.

"What was that about? You seem upset," Andrea said.

"Louis is going meet with us at the café across the street. From the sound of his voice, I think he has something to tell me that I might not like."

"Wait and see what he has to say before you get all wound up." Andrea replied.

Jenna and Andrea met with the detective at the café. The three of them ordered lunch and a café latte each. Jenna sipped on the latte as she waited for Detective Chambeaux to tell her what he had found out. She could feel tension building up at the back of her neck.

"I must say, it has been an interesting but frustrating case so far," Louis began. "I started my investigation with Brandon and then I worked back to Gary."

He pulled out all his reports from his briefcase and began to relay the information he had obtained up to date.

"It turns out Brandon Styles didn't leave any trails that I could get my hands on, and as far as any relatives, there were none—at least, no one that I could trace down at this point in time. I contacted the police department in California where you thought his parents might have lived, but I couldn't get any information on him whatsoever, which seems out of the ordinary. Brandon baffles me. Didn't he ever discuss any previous employment when you were together, or talk about his family members at all?"

"The only thing that I remember him mentioning was that his parents lived somewhere in California, and that he worked for an economics company," Jenna said. "He never talked very much about his family or any other jobs. There were things that he just wouldn't talk about. I never questioned him. I just thought there must have been an important reason for his not wanting to speak about his past."

"Interesting indeed. Did you take care of all the finances?"

"Yes, why? Was there something wrong with that?" Jenna asked with a look of puzzlement.

"I found no records of any financial transactions under the name of Brandon Styles. It's obvious he wanted you to look after all the financial matters for some reason," Louis noted to her.

"I just thought that he didn't like doing bookkeeping," Jenna said, confused.

Louis shook his head. "I hate to say this, Jenna, but I have a strong feeling that there was another reason he left all the financial matters up to you."

"What do you think it was?" she asked again with a surprised expression.

"The more I searched for information on Brandon, the more I began to recognize that he wanted to remain anonymous. If there were any financial transactions at all in his name, I'd have a trail on him by now."

"So, what you're saying, then, is that he lied to me to the whole time we were together," she said, with a dismayed expression.

"It does appear that way. I called the agency you told me about, and they said no one by that name was ever employed there."

"What!" Jenna stopped eating and stared at Louis. "You can't be serious. Wow! That is so mind-boggling. How could I have been so naïve?"

"Did you find anything at all that indicated what Brandon did for a living?" Andrea asked.

No, he is a total conundrum. I think he was leading a double life and covered all his bases so no trail of his affairs would be found. I'll need to delve into this investigation much deeper to find out."

"Oh, my God!" Jenna exclaimed in astonishment. "Do you really think he was leading two different lives?" she asked, not really believing it.

"Yes, Jenna I do. In my experience as a detective, if a person has left little or no trail of his or her transactions and no visible information about past residences, it's usually because they're leading a double life. Most often, these people continually move from place to place to avoid leaving any tracks behind." Louis paused a few moments to allow Jenna to absorb the startling news. He continued, "A more expensive undertaking will be required for me to dig deeper into this matter. I will need help to probe into this situation further, and I will likely need to travel overseas."

"Overseas! Why would you need to go abroad?" Jenna emphatically asked.

"From what I have been able to find out, there have been some unexplained deaths, and disappearances in certain parts of Europe as well, in Germany and the Netherlands and there may be a link there. I have some connections in Germany, which might turn out to be a benefit for this case of yours."

"I see," Jenna said, feeling disheartened. She couldn't say anything else.

"Are you sure you want Louis to carry on with this investigation, Jenna?" Andrea asked. "It might not be worth the hefty expense or the time involved."

"I need to think about it. It's a lot to consider," Jenna said, feeling unsure. "What about Gary? Were you able to get any information on him?" She then asked.

"I found a little more information about Gary than I did for Brandon, but not a great deal. He does have relatives in Vancouver, who I still need to contact, but only if you decide you want me to go on with this quest."

"It's all just so incredible. I can't believe this," Jenna said, turning her head away. "Wow! I knew so little about either one of them. Give me a day to register all of this in my mind."

"I think you need to be completely certain that you want this investigation to be taken further," Louis warned. "It will be costly, and it will take much more time than what you had hoped for. However, what I can do for you right now is hire someone to keep surveillance for a few weeks, to keep a lookout for these characters who have been following you. I would be fine with doing that for a minimal cost."

Jenna felt mentally drained. She stared at Louis, feeling totally overwhelmed. She fidgeted with her hands and glanced around the room, avoiding answering him right away.

"Jenna, speak up. Do you want him to hire someone in the meantime or not?" Andrea asked impatiently.

Taking a deep breath, she said, "Yeah I . . . suppose I should for my own sanity. It would, at least, give me some idea of what's going on and make me feel safer."

"Only if you're certain," Louis strongly stated. "I will arrange for someone to keep an eye on you. I know someone who is highly trained in apprehending stalkers. He will be close by whenever you go anywhere. If anything appears strange or out of the norm, he will immediately consider it."

"What choice do I have if I want to know why I'm being followed?" Jenna said, trying to make her mind up. "I do have some money saved. I'll have to arrange to have it released into my chequing account. I do want the surveillance for now. As far as the rest of the investigation, let me think about it."

"Not a problem. I'm sorry you are going through this, Jenna. It's truly a staggering situation, and if these two men who are following you are somehow tied in with Gary and Brandon, then it may be a good idea that you find out what they were up to."

"I sure didn't expect to hear anything like what you've just told us," Jenna said, clearly upset. "Are you ready to leave?" she asked Andrea as she slipped her coat on. "I'll be in touch with you once I've made my decision," she said to Louis.

"Get back to the centre. I'll call you the minute the security agent is available," he said. With that, the women left.

As they left the café, Jenna looked around to see if anyone followed them—a habit that had been recently imposed upon her.

Jenna and Andrea decided not to shop and set out directly for the women's centre. On the way, there, they stopped at a liquor store to buy more wine for the evening and to rent a couple of movies. Wine was not allowed in their room, but at that point, neither of them cared. Hiding out wasn't something Jenna had planned on doing while living in Paris. So far, her experience had been an exasperating one.

For some reason, that night felt ill-omened to Jenna. Somehow, the cacophony of the busy city didn't have the same appeal as it had originally. The brilliant city lights seemed darkened by the gloom she felt within, which brought back insecurities and fears that she had tried so hard to leave in her past.

Andrea and Jenna settled in, sitting down to have a glass of wine and to watch the movies.

"I want to know what your thoughts are about this whole messy affair before we watch the movies," Jenna said. "My mind is too rattled right now to concentrate on films."

"It's a major decision you have to make. It depends on how much you really want to know the truth, and what you're prepared to spend to find out," Andrea replied.

"Money is a factor. But until I know the truth about Gary and Brandon, will I ever rest? I just can't believe I was so stupid. Tomorrow I'll to go to a bank and find out how much money I have in my account and in my shares that I can cash in right away."

She spent the evening thinking about the ongoing hunt for information on Brandon and Gary. Her thoughts went back and forth between whether she should go ahead with the investigation or not.

CHAPTER FIFTEEN

Jenna and Andrea woke up the following morning to a bright sunny day. It was early enough that the traffic didn't seem to be quite as hectic as it was most of the time. Jenna hoped that it would be a better day all around. She wanted to have breakfast at the café across the street from the centre and then get to the bank as soon as the doors opened.

Once they finished their lovely breakfast, the two women were quick to set out for the bank. Andrea waited in the lobby while Jenna checked her accounts. She looked at all her financial records and saw that there was more money in her accounts than she had realized. Going ahead with the investigation would be fine, if she knew what Louis's fee would be.

"I think I am OK with funds, Andrea," Jenna said as they left the bank. "My grandfather on my father's side of the family left me an inheritance when he passed away five years passed. I invested a good sum of that money. It has done well. I am good to go, as long as I have an idea of approximately how much Louis plans to charge me."

"That's great. Then we should get to his office right now and tell Louis what you have decided."

"I will call him and see if he's available." Jenna took out her cell phone and dialed Louis's number.

"Detective Louis Chambeaux speaking."

"Good morning Louis, it's Jenna. Do you have some time this morning? I've made a decision."

"I do have 11:00 open."

"Great. We have nothing else going on. Andrea and I will be there at 11."

"OK, see you then."

It was 10:00 when they arrived outside Louis's office, which meant they had an hour to pass before the meeting.

"Why don't we go have a cup of coffee at one of the other cafés around here?" Jenna suggested.

As they began crossing the street toward the café bistro, Jenna shuddered. She spotted a man sitting in a parked car just a few doorways down from the café. With her voice rising in panic, she said to Andrea. "I think that same man from the restaurant is back, he's sitting in that parked car over there, look!"

"Are you sure it's him?" Andrea asked as she looked around.

"Just look for yourself," Jenna said, almost screeching.

Andrea glanced over to the parked car. "I think you're right. He does look like the same person. Let's cross over to the other side, now."

As they briskly crossed to the other side of the street, Jenna asked, "How do these men know what we're doing? It seems like no matter where we are, one of them is following us."

"Yeah, I'd like to know that, too," Andrea agreed.

Not far from Chambeaux's office building was another small café. Jenna was upset and feeling weak, she needed to sit down.

"You're not looking very well right now. Don't get yourself in a knot about this," Andrea said.

Andrea ordered a coffee and Jenna just stared out the window, watching to see if the man still tailed them.

After a quick coffee, it was 10:45, Jenna and Andrea set out for the detective's office. Even though they were fifteen minutes early, they didn't mind waiting in the lobby; they were happy to be out of that man's sight.

Jenna's breathing was laboured. She sat on a bench and took a couple of deep breaths.

"Are you alright, Jenna? Do you want a glass of water" Andrea asked?

"Yes, water, please," Jenna replied, panting slightly.

Andrea walked over to the receptionist and asked if she could have a glass of water for her friend. The woman didn't hesitate, noticing that Jenna seemed distressed.

Louis opened his office door and walked out at 11:00 sharp. Right away he saw that Jenna appeared troubled.

"Ladies, please, come in. Is something wrong Jenna? You look pale."

"I saw the same man sitting in a parked car just down the street. It was a little difficult to see in the car, but. . ." Jenna paused, trying to hold back the tears. "I'm pretty sure it was him."

"Maybe because you're distraught you think you saw this person?" Louis asked as the three of them sat down in his office.

"No!" She said, loudly. "Andrea thought it was the same person, too. How do these men know what we're doing?"

"I wish I knew the answer," Louis said.

"In any case, I've decided that you should continue with the investigation, but I need to know what it will cost," Jenna said, as she tried to calm herself down.

"It will probably run several thousands of dollars. It will depend on how fast I can obtain the information I need. And if I need to travel overseas, that will bring the cost up more, of course."

"Then, you know what, I must know, go ahead. In the meantime, will you have someone watch over us?" Jenna tensely asked.

"Yes, I have already arranged it. Marcel will be there by mid-afternoon tomorrow. He will stand watch for the better part of the day. I told him the particulars so that he has an idea of what he's up against."

"That's a relief, thank you."

"I know it won't be easy for you. Meanwhile, try and relax," Louis said.

"Thank you again for all your help, Detective Chambeaux," Jenna said with bated breath. "I'll be waiting to hear from you. I trust you will get to the bottom of this whole mysterious business soon."

"I sure hope so," the detective replied. "And please, call me Louis."

"Call me as soon as you can, Louis," Jenna said. She and Andrea left his office feeling a little less fearful knowing there would be someone there

CHAPTER SIXTEEN

After receiving Jenna's go-ahead to continue with the investigation, Louis immediately resumed his search. He called a number in Vancouver that he was given for a Thompson family.

"Hello, this is the Thompson residence," a woman answered.

"Hello, Mrs. Thompson. My name is Detective Louis Chambeaux from Paris, France. You're probably wondering why a detective from France is calling you. It's in regards to a man named Gary Thompson. Would he be relative of yours?"

She was silent for a few moments. "A detective! Oh, my Lord! You have completely caught me off guard. Gary is my son . . . but my husband and I haven't seen him in years. He disappeared in 1995. We assumed he died and that his body was never found. It's been so devastating, to say the least. . . but since then, I've lost my husband as well."

"I'm so sorry for your loss, Mrs. Thompson. I had no idea. I must tell you, Gary did die, but not long ago, in Alberta. There seems to be a real mystery surrounding his death. I was hired by his wife, Jenna, to consider this matter."

"What? I can't believe what you're saying. He was alive, and married! I need to sit down . . . my legs are buckling."

"This must be terribly shocking to you, and I'm sorry you had to find out this way," Louis said.

"There are no words that I can say, except that I'm shocked. I accepted that he was gone, but to hear this now is unbelievable."

"That's quite understandable, Mrs. Thompson. I'm surprised, as well, that you thought he was dead all this time. Would it be convenient for you if we arrange a meeting sometime soon so that I may get more information about your son Gary?"

"I suppose not. Give me a couple of days. I need to wrap my mind around what you have just told me."

"How about we meet at the end of next week?" Louis asked. "Would that be suitable?"

"Yes, I think that would be fine. Call a day before just to confirm."

"Alright, then I shall call you in a few days, and we'll set up a time when it is convenient."

"Goodbye." Mrs. Thompson hung up the phone, leaving Louis stunned.

I've dealt with strange situations before, he thought, *but this one is a doozy.*

* * *

Until his meeting with Mrs. Thompson the next step on Louis's list was to continue investigating Brandon. He did some extensive research on the Internet, hoping to come across information about Brandon's past activities, but he found it to be a waste of time.

Louis's connections, which he had established in London, England, Germany, the Netherlands, and Switzerland, would be a great asset to this investigation. He planned on contacting the people he knew in all those countries.

For the next few days, he devoted his time to finding out what he could about Brandon's past activities, starting in Denmark. Telephone calls went going back and forth, and he obtained some startling revelations from undercover investigators he knew.

Louis found out that Brandon went by a different name while working with some type of secretive organization in Amsterdam, called Nebula's Moon. A group of international investigators are considering this organization's activities.

Louis was given a name of a contact in Germany, a man who had befriended Brandon when he was a member of this same association as well, and Louis called this person. Apparently, this man who knew Brandon overheard him speaking one day via video to someone about his involvement with a woman named Jenna. He remembered Brandon saying, "as soon as I have what I want, I'll be in touch." The man told Louis that he didn't quite understand what Brandon meant by that, but from the sound of the discussion between him and the person on the video, he felt that this woman Jenna might be in grave danger. He decided to transmit what he overheard to the police authorities, on the condition that his affiliation with the organization would not be disclosed. The police then turned the information over to a secret agency.

Louis asked the man if he knew anything about a Gary Thompson and if perhaps he was involved as well. He described Gary to the person, to whom he was speaking with.

He told Louis that there was a man named Gary Thompson involved with the organization, but his name was spelled "Thomson" without the "p."

Louis was dumbfounded. He now knew he was on to something very covert. There were shadowy aspects about these two men Jenna had married, and he was almost certain that Brandon was a person of interest in this organization.

He arranged an immediate flight to Denmark. He wanted to arrange a meeting with a man named Hans.

CHAPTER SEVENTEEN

Jenna and Andrea waited patiently at the centre to hear back from Louis. They stayed in more than they went out, and when they did venture away from the women's centre, the security agent, Marcel, was only a few yards behind them.

They decided to help with some of the daily chores while staying at the centre. They were each given a task to do every day, whether it was cooking, cleaning, or running errands. Jenna and Andrea chose to do outside errands whenever something was required. It gave them a chance to get away from the environment of the women's shelter and to enjoy a good cup of café latte at a café. The coffee at the centre wasn't that great.

Jenna and Andrea had been at the facility for nearly two weeks, and all was calm as far as they knew. Whoever followed them in the past must have known that someone was looking after their safety and ceased. They never saw anyone skulking about whenever they left the place.

Louis called Marcel to ask how things were going with the situation. Marcel was a thickset man with large hands and wide shoulders. He had been a wrestler up until he became involved with doing stakeouts for the police department, and Louis felt that Marcel would be someone that could help make Jenna and Andrea feel safer.

"It's been quiet since you left. I haven't come across anyone suspicious, yet," Marcel said.

"Maybe whoever these guys are know the women are being looked after," Louis commented.

"You could be right," Marcel replied. "How much longer will you need me to do this stakeout?"

"Let's give it one more week. I think I'm getting somewhere with this investigation. There was a lot more was going on with these two men Jenna was married to, more than she ever knew or realized."

"I'm not surprised. Let me know when you plan on coming back to Paris. In the meantime, I'll keep you posted on any developments."

"OK, talk soon."

After hanging hung up the phone, Louis then thought to opened another investigation on Gary, but he decided that Brandon was the more secretive of the two. He called his contact as soon as he arrived in Denmark. They arranged to meet at an off-the-beaten-track bar so they could talk in private.

Hans, a tall, thin man, waited for Louis at the bar. He had some information to share with him.

"Goedemorgen," Hans said to Louis as he sat down.

"Goedemorgen, Hans. Have you any information for me about this man, Brandon Styles?"

"Ja, I do. This man Brandon Styles apparently was involved with a secret society not far from Amsterdam, called Nebula's Moon. He was the leader of this association. It is not a large group from what I have been able to determine. Our department has been watching them for a while now. For some reason, no one we spoke to about this organization knew much about them, except that they're not originally from, Amsterdam or Germany, but from somewhere else. And from what I've gathered, this establishment wants to stay in the shadows." Hans paused for a moment to take a sip of his beer before continuing. He appeared quite pensive.

"Another thing that might be of interest to you is that not long ago, two agents from the Denmark secret agency disappeared, and their whereabouts are unknown to this day. They were doing some investigating on Styles at the time. Whether they are still alive or not, we don't know. That is still being considered."

"Oh, really? Whoa!" Louis exclaimed. "Now that is not just coincidental."

Hans nodded, looking grim. "I also found out that this Brandon character tried to speak to the assistant to the Prime Minister of the Netherlands; something about an important change that will affect all of humanity."

Louis moved closer in to the table so no one in the bar could hear what he was saying. Louis's eyes widened and he quietly asked, "What is that supposed to mean, it will affect all of humanity?"

"I don't know. This fellow that I spoke with didn't say any more than that. I personally think this Styles guy might have been an undercover agent for some other country. Russia, perhaps, but I can't say for sure."

"A spy! Ah, yes, I suspected that he might be leading a double life. It would make sense since I couldn't find any records of any of his activities in Canada or the US, where supposedly his family resided. However, I did obtain some of the same information that you have." Louis vigorously rubbed his chin, untied his tie as though he was feeling hot, and momentarily stared out into the room.

"Styles was obviously trying to warn the assistant," Hans added.

With a concerned expression, Louis looked at Hans. "That is very interesting information about him. Is this guy's life some kind of riddle, or what?"

"I wish I could help you more, but that's all the information I was given." Hans said. "There is someone else who might be able to give you more data about this man, Brandon. Here is his business card. He lives in Germany."

Louis looked at the name on the card. It said Gunter Bergman, SFA.

"Thank you, Hans. You have given me a lot more information than I wasn't able to attain on my own. I will contact Gunter Bergman right away."

"Good luck, Louis. I hope you can get to the bottom of this whole mystery."

"That would be nice. Thank you again, Hans. Bye for now," Louis said, firmly shaking hands with Hans.

"Please let me know what else you find out. I would be very interested in knowing," Hans said.

"I will," Louis said, and he left the bar.

There were so many questions going through Louis's mind as he walked out, but at least he had a few more details about Brandon Styles.

CHAPTER EIGHTEEN

Well over two weeks had gone by since Louis left for Denmark. Jenna and Andrea still hadn't heard from him. They were getting concerned and wondered if something had happened to him.

They were tired of staying indoors and decided to go out for dinner one evening. They went to inform the supervisor they were going out for dinner when the assistant approached them to say there was a phone call for Jenna.

Jenna picked up the phone, "Hello?"

"Hi, Jenna, it's Louis. How are things? Have there been any new developments since we last spoke?"

"It's so nice to hear from you, Louis," Jenna said, looking at Andrea with a pleased expression on her face. "Andrea and I were just wondering about you. No, nothing else has happened since you left, but I think Marcel is getting tired of standing by."

"Yeah, he probably needs a break. I have attained some info from a man I spoke with in Denmark. I will need to travel to Hamburg, Germany next. I am flying out in a couple of days. I'll give you a call as soon as I am settled in."

"Great, Louis. Thanks for calling."

Jenna hung up and told Andrea the news. "I hope whatever he found out will be worthwhile."

"Me too." Andrea agreed.

As they headed out for dinner, they saw Marcel standing close by.

"Hi, Marcel," Jenna waved as they approached him. "I just got a call from Louis. He's planning on flying to Germany to do more investigating. I think you could probably cease this watch if you wish."

"I think I will stay put for one more day. If there's still no sign of anyone shadowing you, then I will call it a day."

"Thank you very much for being here. It hasn't been a positive stay for me in Paris, so far. I wasn't expecting all of this to happen."

"Totally understandable, Jenna. Whoever these men are . . . maybe they have decided to stop following you. I haven't seen anyone suspicious prowling about since I started," Marcel replied.

With a heavy breath, out, Jenna said, "Perhaps." She wasn't convinced. "In any case, we want to be able to move around freely and not have to worry about anyone creeping around us."

"Are you going somewhere right now?"

"We're going out for dinner. It's been over two weeks since we went out anywhere."

"Very well. I will keep watch this evening," Marcel said, and he followed them from a distance.

Jenna and Andrea decided to try a new restaurant that evening. They chose an oriental restaurant not far from the center. The food sounded delicious. They crossed over a boulevard to get to the restaurant. Marcel walked a few yards behind them. As he followed them across, he noticed a man standing just inside an alleyway not far from the restaurant. The man was dressed in a one-piece black uniform style outfit, just like Jenna and Andrea had described on the men who were following them. Marcel stopped. He waited to see if the man was going to follow the women. Sure enough, he stepped out from the alleyway as soon as Jenna and Andrea neared the restaurant, and Marcel began to pursue him. Jenna and Andrea entered the diner, not knowing they were being tailed.

Marcel immediately advanced on the man. The man saw Marcel approaching and dashed into another laneway. The chase began. Marcel ran as fast he could after the uniformed man down the alley, losing him for a couple of minutes. He figured that he had gone down a connecting alley and followed that one. The black-clothed man kept zig-zagging in out of different passageways, but once Marcel caught sight of him, he didn't lose sight of him again. Marcel was a fast runner, but the man moved like a cougar. The stalker reached a wall that closed off the last alley they entered, but like a daddy-long-legged spider, he climbed up the wall with no difficulties. Marcel was starting to lose his breath, and just as he reached to grab hold of the man's leg, the mysterious character pulled out what appeared to be a gun. Suddenly, a blazing beam of light hit Marcel in the chest, and he fell to the ground, unconscious. The man completely vanished from sight.

A little while later, a homeless person walking in the laneway found Marcel passed out. He ran to the nearest convenience store and asked the clerk to call an ambulance. Marcel was immediately taken to the hospital.

* * *

While all of this was occurring, Jenna and Andrea were enjoying their dinner and talking about Marcel. They discussed their concerns about him leaving his watch over them, but they also accepted that he would not be there for them after that evening.

"I hope Louis will have some information soon, because if Marcel isn't going to be watching anymore, we're open targets again," Jenna said with angst.

"I know. Let's just enjoy our meals and not talk about it anymore for tonight. Louis should be back sometime soon," Andrea replied.

When they left the restaurant, they noticed that Marcel wasn't where he was supposed to be. They glanced around to see if they could spot him, but he was nowhere close by.

"I wonder where he went," Jenna said. "He said he would do the stakeout for one more night. . ."

"Maybe he needed to use a bathroom," Andrea responded.

They were both feeling tired and decided to return to their room to have a night cap before settling in for the night.

The night was clear and calm, and they decided to take a chance and walk instead of hailing a cab. The centre was not as close as they thought, but they walked the whole way back anyway. Luckily for them, no one followed.

CHAPTER NINETEEN

Marcel was not in good condition, but the doctor who examined him thought he would pull through if he kept a close eye on his recovery. The doctor called the investigation department to notify them that Marcel was in the hospital with a serious injury from what he thought to be an attempt made on his life.

The inspector who answered immediately arranged to have the matter considered and to have someone visit Marcel as soon as possible. There had been a similar incident just recently with another agent, who was also doing a stakeout for someone else. He was now convinced that something unusual was occurring. He felt that it had become even more urgent for him to get to the bottom of these actions.

Meanwhile, Louis planned on heading back to Paris from the Netherlands and arranged a flight within the next day. He was anxious to speak with Jenna and Andrea to tell them about some of the details that he had attained about Gary and Brandon. His suspicions about the two men being underhanded characters were not unfounded.

Louis called Marcel on his cell phone, but he got only his answering service in response. He didn't give it much thought at the time; he would try him again later.

The plane was making its descent when Louis tried Marcel again, and still there was no answer. It seemed odd for Marcel not to answer or return his calls. Louis wondered if something had gone wrong. The fact that Marcel wasn't answering his calls really concerned him.

Once he had arrived at the baggage area, Louis tried Marcel's phone once again, but still nothing. He needed to get to his office right away to find out what was going on. His main concern was for Jenna's and Andrea's safety.

As soon as he got into his office, he called the investigation department, hoping they would know of Marcel's whereabouts.

"Hello, this is Louis Chambeaux. Is the inspector in? I need to speak with him."

"One moment Detective Chambeaux, I will put you through," the secretary replied.

"Inspector Allain Croteau."

"Inspector Croteau, its Louis Chambeaux. Do you by chance know of Marcel's whereabouts? I've tried his cell phone a few times, and I'm not getting any answer."

"I'm glad you called, Louis. Unfortunately, Marcel is in the hospital with a serious injury. We think there was an attempt made on his life. He was doing a stakeout for clients of yours, was he not?"

"Yes, he was. *Damn it!* I suspected something was up when he didn't answer his phone. Was he shot?"

"Not with a gun. The doctor examining Marcel concluded that he was hit by a beam of light coming from some sort of projectile, which knocked him unconscious, causing him injury. We still don't understand what this projectile was exactly. The doctor thinks he has a good chance of coming out of it OK. I'm having a couple of my agents investigating this affair. We need to get to the bottom of these violations. They could very well be the actions of a sophisticated organization. He's very lucky he wasn't killed."

"Yeah, what in hell is going on? Can I see him, or will I have to wait for a few days?" Louis was clearly troubled; he nervously tapped his pen on his desk while speaking with the inspector.

"I think it would be best to give it a day or so before you visit him. I'll be in touch with you once I know for sure when it would be a good time for him to have visitors," The inspector replied.

Louis was beside himself about what happened to Marcel, and that incident made him more alarmed. He hadn't expected any of this to happen.

"OK, I'll wait to hear from you. Call me as soon as it's clear for me to see him," Louis said, feeling very uneasy.

"Will do," Croteau replied.

Louis hung up the phone, grabbed a beer from his tiny refrigerator, and sat down on his leather sofa. He needed to get his thoughts together before calling the women. This situation was now, without any doubt, much more severe than he had original thought it would be. *Will I be able to get someone else to help me with these states of affairs or not?* he wondered.

He decided he had to say something to Jenna and Andrea about the current state of affairs, but not everything he knew. It would all be much too disturbing, especially for Jenna.

Stroking the growing bristles on his chin, Louis thought, *I need to shave before morning.*

"This whole case is incredibly stupefying," he said aloud, yanking at a clump of his hair. "I need time to think about these obscure events that are going on to get a better perspective on things, so I can move forward with the investigation."

CHAPTER TWENTY

Louis arrived in Paris in the evening. He woke up at the crack of dawn the next morning, anxious to speak with Jenna and Andrea. He also needed to find out how Marcel was doing.

"Hello, this is Jenna speaking," Jenna answered when he called.

"Hi, Jenna, it's Louis."

"Hi, you're calling early. We're still in bed. We were just talking about you."

"I'm sorry. I know it's early. Are you available this morning, say around 10:30?"

"10:30 should be fine. Do you have some information for us?"

"Yes, I do have some information to share with you. I think you'll be surprised at what I have found out. Another bad incident has occurred, which I will tell you about when we meet."

"Oh! Oh! That doesn't sound good," Jenna replied, sounding alarmed.

"Unfortunately, it isn't. I'll see you at 10:30."

"OK, we'll be waiting." Jenna could feel tension building in her shoulders as she hung up the phone.

Andrea yawned. "Ahhh! That was Louis, I gather? What did he say? You seem grim, suddenly."

Jenna's expression was restrained. "From what Louis said, it doesn't sound good, Andrea. He said he had information, and there was a bad incident that he needed to tell us about."

"Wait and see what he has to say before you get your underwear all up in a knot," Andrea replied, trying to keep Jenna from getting all worked up.

The buzzer rang at exactly 10:30. The custodian answered. "Yes, how can I help you?"

"It's Detective Chambeaux. I have an appointment with Jenna and Andrea this morning at 10:30. Could you notify them that I'm here?"

"Yes, Detective Chambeaux, I will ring their room." She called their room.

"Yes, this is Andrea."

"Detective Chambeaux is here. He says he has an appointment with you this morning."

"Yes, he does. Please let him in, thank you," Andrea answered.

"You may go up, Detective."

Jenna stood at the door waiting for Louis to knock. As soon as he came in, Jenna could tell by the look on his face that he didn't have positive news.

"We have some coffee made. Would you care to have a cup?" she offered him.

"Sure. I could use some caffeine, thanks."

Jenna poured each of them a cup of coffee. As he sat on the sofa, Louis proceeded to tell them some of the information he had found out about Brandon when he spoke with a man in Denmark and from his contact in Germany, and the bad news about Marcel. He didn't know how to tell them about what had happened to Marcel in a gentler way, so he told them like it was. Jenna and Andrea both looked at each other in astonishment.

"I know what you're feeling and thinking. I certainly didn't expect him to be injured in the process. This situation is a lot more involved than I initially thought it to be," Louis said, realizing how it must have sounded to Jenna and Andrea.

"I'm totally speechless, Louis," Jenna said. "I don't know what to say. It's beyond anything that I would have imagined about Brandon, and what's happened to Marcel is horrible." Jenna got up from where she sat, walked to the small kitchenette, poured another cup of coffee, and stood by the sink, bewildered.

"Jenna, come sit down," Andrea said.

With a downcast expression, Jenna sat back down on the sofa. "I feel like I'm in a twilight zone. I feel so awful about Marcel."

"Yes, it's too bad what happened to him. I was told that he'll pull through it OK, though. Unfortunately, sometimes risks like this are part of the job, but I never expected it to happen to him. It was a man in a black outfit. He used a laser type of weapon, which shot out a light beam, hitting Marcel in the chest."

"Wow! This sounds like something out of the Star Trek movie," Andrea said anxiously.

"What's going on, Louis? This is getting more and more frightening each time we speak with you," Jenna said in her high-strung tone. "How much more can I take?" Almost in tears, she put her head down.

"I know it's bizarre, and I understand how terrifying this must be for you. In view of what happened to Marcel, do you still want me to continue with the inquiries? My next step was to fly to Hamburg, Germany. I was given the name of a person to contact there that apparently has more information on Brandon."

"I'm too shaken up right now, Louis. I can't give you answer right now," Jenna replied, not lifting her head.

"Think about it for a day and get back to me with your answer. If you decide that you want me to go on with it, it's important not to waste too much time. In the meantime, I'll check on Marcel."

"I need some time to think about everything that you've told us. Keep us posted about Marcel, please."

"I will. I realize that anything I say to you right now won't be enough to ease your mind." Louis wasn't feeling the greatest himself after telling them about Marcel's incident.

"I'll see that she tries to calm down," Andrea said, rubbing her friend's back.

"Alright then, I'll be in touch. In view of what has taken place, I would suggest you both stay put for now," Louis said firmly.

"I don't think we'll be venturing out very far. It's much too scary to even consider right now," Jenna stated. She felt most disturbed about what had happened to Marcel, and she considered herself responsible for the incident.

After Louis left, Jenna poured herself a large glass of wine and sat on the chair, not uttering a word.

"Do you want to know what my thoughts are?" Andrea asked.

"Yes, of course. Tell me?"

"Personally, I would forget about all of this. The situation is getting worse. The investigation seems to be inviting greater danger to you and for the people who are trying to help. I think it's time to walk away from it, leave well enough alone, and go back home to Alberta."

"I know what you're saying, but what about the men who are doing these horrible things? If they aren't stopped, what else will they do?"

"I think Louis and the others will probably continue to investigate without you, knowing what they know now."

"You're probably right. This case is much too baffling for Louis not to carry on with it."

"That's what I think. Take the day to think about it. Meanwhile, I should make a call to my boss to let him know when I plan to be home. I won't be able to stay much longer."

"I understand.'' Jenna got up from the couch, feeling overwhelmed. She walked around the living room, agonizing about her situation. Tears welled up in her eyes.

Andrea stepped into the other room to make her call while Jenna stood by the window, looking out. She felt confused, angry, and sad all at once. *What will it take to help me make a sound decision, knowing the present state of affairs.*

CHAPTER TWENTY-ONE

Andrea's boss told her he needed her at work when she called him; there were some important papers that he required for a critical meeting coming up. Things had gotten hectic since she left, and now it was time for her to get back to her job.

She looked at Jenna with regretful eyes. "Well, Jenna, I'm sorry to say, but my boss says he needs me at the office. He can't afford for me to be away from my job much longer. I have no choice in the matter, and I'll need to get back within the week."

"I know, and I'm really sorry you won't be getting any more holidays this year. Thank you. It was great to have you here with me. I'll miss you, but I do understand."

* * *

The next morning while having breakfast, Andrea asked Jenna, "Have you decided to have Louis continue with the investigation?"

"I want to give it more thought. However, I think I'll ask him to do some checking in Germany. If it doesn't produce anything that will give me a better idea of what Brandon and Gary were involved with, then I'll forget about it and go home."

"It's up to you, but I think you're wasting your time, energy, and money. What's in the past shouldn't have any bearing on what you'll be doing in the future."

"Yes, you're right. Nevertheless, maybe I need to give it at least one more try."

"Well, in any case, I have to arrange a flight home for next Friday. That gives us a few more days to spend some time together." Andrea gave her a big hug. She felt sad for Jenna.

"You've been a good friend, Andrea. I couldn't have gone through this all without you." She put her head-on Andrea's shoulder.

After a few moments, Jenna finally pulled herself together and said, "That's enough moping. I think I'll call Louis in the morning and tell him my decision."

● * *

Jenna was up early the next morning and made a call to Louis. She left a message saying that she had decided and to call her back.

"I have an idea," Andrea announced. "Why don't we ask Louis if he would consider going out to dinner with us? That would be a nice send off for me, and we wouldn't be alone."

"That's a good idea. I'll ask him when he calls me back. I really like Louis, and it might give me a chance to get to know him a bit better. It's too bad I had to meet him under these circumstances."

"Are you getting a bit smitten with him, mmm?" Andrea asked, grinning.

"Maybe," Jenna replied coyly.

They spent most of the morning talking about everything that happened in the past few months. They planned to make reservations for three at a nice restaurant. They were sure Louis would go out to dinner with them.

It was mid-afternoon when Louis returned the call. "Hi, Jenna. Have you made a decision?"

"Yes. Andrea and I were just talking, and we thought it might be nice for the three of us to have dinner at a nice restaurant tomorrow evening. We could talk about my decision over dinner. Andrea must go back to work in a few days, and it would be a nice send off for her. What do you think, would you be up to doing that?"

"Yeah, sure. I know of a great little place. I'll make the reservations. I know the owner, and he will give us preferential treatment."

"Great. How does 7:00 sound?"

"Perfect. I will pick you up around 6:30, which will give us plenty of time."

"See you then."

"It will be nice to just relax over dinner for a change," Andrea said as Jenna hung up the phone.

"Yes, it will. Let's go through what clothes we have to wear." Jenna felt a bit calmer about having dinner out with Louis there.

It had been a while since either of them dressed up in fancier clothes. They both tried their clothes on. Jenna chose a slim fitting light blue dress with a plunging neckline, and Andrea chose a burgundy skirt with a lacy white top. Looking in the mirror after they were dressed, they knuckle punched each other.

"You look stunning, Ms. Jenna."

"And you look gorgeous, Ms. Andrea." They kidded around, trying to lighten things up.

Louis was right on time the next evening. He rang the supervisor to say he was visiting the women and then called them on his cell phone.

Andrea answered, "Hello? Is that you, Louis?"

"Yes, I'll wait in the car out front," he said, looking out the car window.

"We'll be right down," Andrea said.

Louis had made reservations at a classy restaurant, known for its delicious food and excellent service. Musicians played violins as the patrons ate and talked. It was an elegant setting. Jenna and Andrea had never been to a restaurant that provided live music before.

"Ladies, I hope you like the restaurant I have chosen. It's one of the best in the area. The food is fabulous, and whatever you choose, I'm confident you will enjoy it."

The waiter wore a bow tie and came to the table with a white cloth draped over his arm. He asked them in French if they would like to see the menu. Louis answered, "Oui, sil vous plait."

"Tres bons, Detective Chambeaux."

Paris was glamorous in so many ways. Jenna and Andrea felt as though they were in a movie scene, sitting somewhere exotic.

They each selected something different to eat from the French menu, asking Louis for his recommendations. It was difficult for them to make their choices; everything on the menu sounded delicious.

As they waited for their dinner to be served, Louis asked Jenna if she had made up her mind about him continuing the inquiries on Brandon and Gary.

"I've thought about everything that you told us, and I think you should continue with your search in Germany. If it doesn't turn out to be any more beneficial, then I'll discontinue this whole investigation."

"If you're certain that you want me to go on with it, then I'll get back at it as soon as I can. What will you do? Will you stay at the centre after Andrea goes home?"

"Yes, I think that would be best for me, for a while at least. I'll try and limit the time I go out. Maybe I'll help some of the other women with their issues."

"That's a great idea. I will see if I can get someone else to do the watch, perhaps not as extensive as what Marcel did, but I'd like to have someone there for some of the times you're are out and about, at least. Marcel is recovering and should be out of the hospital in about a week. I still need to speak to him about what happened. I didn't get an opportunity to go over the incident with him, yet."

"I still shake inside when I think about it," Jenna said, still feeling upset about what happened to Marcel.

"Yeah, me, too. That was totally freaky," Andrea agreed.

"Here's our dinner, let's enjoy it. No more talking about that episode for tonight," Louis responded as the waiter placed their dishes on the table.

"I need to go to the ladies' room before we eat," Jenna said. She got up and walked to the back of the restaurant where the washrooms were situated. Soft music played in the background and a lovely gardenia scent permeated the air as she walked toward the facility. She was amazed.

An assistant waited inside to provide patrons with anything they required, like a small tube of hand lotion, for example. She handed Jenna a towel once she was out of the cubicle. Jenna was quite impressed by all the niceties that this restaurant provided. Thanking the woman, she walked out.

As she was about to turn the corner on her way back to their table, a vaporous image suddenly appeared down the hallway. A rippling effect filled the air as the image moved forward.

Jenna gasped and, nearly fainting, braced herself against the wall. Gary's image was in the vapour—he was summoning to her to come forth. Then the cloud disappeared as fast as it had appeared. She trembled as she gripped the wooden bar attached to the wall. Quietly, she spoke aloud, "Gary?! Oh! My God! Was that really him? No, no, that's impossible, he's dead. It's just my imagination, again." For several minutes, she clung to the railing, trying to steady herself.

Andrea began to wonder what was keeping Jenna so long. "She's been gone too long," she said to Louis. "I'll go check to see if she is alright."

"It does seem like she's been gone a while. Tell her dinner is here, and it'll get cold if we don't eat soon."

As soon as Andrea stepped around the corner, she noticed Jenna feebly trying to stand while clutching the bar. Her complexion was a pasty white.

"Jenna, what happened? You look as if you've seen a ghost!"

Jenna was hyperventilating. "Let me catch my breath," she said, inhaling and exhaling with quick sequences. "Gary's. . ."

"What! Oh! Come on, Jenna, really! Your mind is doing some strange things again. Understandable, considering what has occurred. But come on, dinner is getting cold; you should have something to eat."

"I know it's totally nuts to think that I actually saw him. I could swear it was him, Andrea, really."

Andrea held onto Jenna's arm as they walked back to the table. "Jenna, listen to me. There are no such things as ghosts. You have been through so much these past few months and I think your mind is conjuring things that aren't there."

As Louis watched them walking toward the table, he thought that Jenna didn't look well.

"Are you alright? Did something happen while you were in the washroom?" he asked, concerned.

"Yes . . . you're not going to believe me," Jenna replied, shaking.

"Try me."

She told him what she saw, or what she thought she saw. Eyes widening, Louis glanced over at Andrea with a questioning expression on his face. Andrea knew exactly what he was thinking.

Louis, trying to be gentle with her, said, "Jenna, I think this whole affair is causing you a lot of stress, and your mind is fabricating images that aren't there."

"You're right. It's my mind playing tricks. Let's eat." Deep down, she couldn't deny how she was feeling, but she thought it best not to say any more.

Louis called for the waiter and asked if he could have their food warmed up. The waiter shrugged his shoulders as though questioning why, but he did what was asked of him. Louis and Andrea finished their dinner, but Jenna just picked at the food in front of her. The mood of the anticipated joyous evening had changed.

Louis suggested that Jenna should perhaps go back to the centre and rest. He'd call her in the morning to see how she was doing.

There were no objections from Jenna or Andrea; they agreed to go back to the women's facility.

Jenna was angry with herself for spoiling their evening.
What a ridiculous idea, saying I saw Gary, she thought. *I must be delirious.*

As they settled in their room for the night, Jenna apologized to Andrea. "I'm so sorry for ruining the evening for you and Louis. I hope I can make it up to you some time."

"Don't worry about it, Jenna. You're mentally and emotionally strained. Our minds can play tricks on us when we're overly stressed."

"I need a night cap and then I'm going to bed. Tomorrow will be a better day, right?"

"It will be," Andrea replied, feeling uncertain.

CHAPTER TWENTY-TWO

Jenna stayed up all night thinking about and questioning the apparition she saw. It had seemed real. Something very strange was happening around her, and all unsettling. Even though she felt that it would be wiser to let it go, she had a niggling need to know what really happened to Gary and Brandon. After seeing what she thought was Gary's ghost, any logical thinking she made have had disappeared.

The next morning, Jenna got up before Andrea. She wanted to go for a walk to clear her mind. It was still dusk and much too early to let the supervisor know she was leaving the centre. It didn't matter; she needed to get outdoors.

Walking along the boulevard helped to take her mind off things, at least for a time. She thought about Louis going to Germany to continue the investigation, and she wondered if she should forget about everything and try to make the best of her situation living in Paris. But she didn't know how she could let any of it go. It seemed that something was compelling her to seek the truth.

She had been walking for an hour when she realized that there was no one keeping an eye on her, and she hurried to get back. As she rushed toward the centre, she noticed a man standing behind some bushes. He stepped out just as she went by. His body radiated like shiny metal. With an alarming hand gesture, he mumbled some words in a language she didn't understand. Terrified, she ran as fast as she could toward the centre.

In the meantime, Andrea woke up and noticed Jenna was gone. She put on a robe and hurried downstairs, but she couldn't find Jenna anywhere. As panic started to set in, she went to speak with the supervisor.

"Excuse me, but have you seen Jenna this morning?" she asked, wringing her hands. "I didn't hear her leave."

"No, not this morning. I just got up," Marianne replied.

"I'm really concerned about her. She's not in a good frame of mind right now," Andrea said fretfully.

"Oh, dear. Can I help in some way?"

"I'll go out and see if I can find her. Could you call Detective Chambeaux and tell him that Jenna is missing and ask him to come here as soon as possible? I may need his help."

"Yes, I can do that."

"Thank you," Andrea responded and quickly went out the door to look for Jenna. Jenna was on her way back to the women's complex when Andrea saw her walking along the boulevard.

"Jenna! What's the matter with you? Why didn't you wake me up to tell me you were going out?" Andrea called out, running toward her friend. "I was frantic thinking something happened to you. You're not supposed to leave the centre without telling the supervisor where you're going!"

"I know. I'm sorry. You were fast asleep and I didn't want to disturb you. I had to get out and clear my mind. I didn't sleep a wink last night, again." Her face was pale and sweat beaded on her forehead.

"Look at you, you're all stirred up," Andrea said, taking Jenna's hand. "You should know better. I realize everything is troubling you, but please, don't do that again."

Jenna trembled at the thought of the character who came out from the bushes. She couldn't tell Andrea what happened. She knew she would be angry at her foolishness.

"I told the supervisor to call Louis. I didn't know what to think. He'll probably be at the centre soon," Andrea said.

"I'm not with it too much these days, am I? I apologize."

"Let's get a coffee to take back with us and wait for Louis. Have you thought any more about him going to Germany?"

"Yes. I've been thinking about everything. That's why I went out," Jenna responded, as the two of them headed toward the café. "For some reason, I have this pesky need to know the truth about Gary and Brandon. I know it's idiotic of me, but I must know. Otherwise, I don't think I'll ever be able to rest easy again."

"You can be so annoyingly persistent, can't you?" Andrea said.

"What can I say?" Jenna replied.

One of the bistro cafés on their way opened early, and they stopped in to get coffees. In the interim, Marianne, the supervisor had placed a call to Louis. He had just woken up when the phone rang.

"Good morning, Detective Chambeaux. I'm sorry to call you so early. Andrea has asked me to call you. Jenna was not in her room when Andrea woke up this morning. She's very concerned about her and would like you to come here as soon as possible." Marianne paused a moment. "Jenna should have let someone know where she was going."

"Good grief, what was she thinking?" Louis wondered out loud. "I'll be there shortly."

"I will let Andrea know you're on your way," Marianne replied and hung up.

CHAPTER TWENTY-THREE

Jenna and Andrea arrived at the building just as Louis pulled up. "I'll see you both inside," he said through the car window, glaring at Jenna.

Jenna and Andrea waited in the lobby. Louis's gait was stiff as he walked in. "What were you thinking, Jenna?"

"I know. I wasn't thinking," she replied, feeling ashamed about worrying everyone.

"No, you weren't. Until all this business is solved, it's important for you to be careful always, especially when you leave the centre. I can't emphasize it any stronger to you. Always let someone know when you're going out. Chances are that these men are probably still around without you realizing it." He took a deep breath to calm himself. "Now, aside from that issue, have you decided about my continuing with the search in Germany?"

"Yes, I have. I won't rest until I have a better idea of what Gary and Brandon were involved in. I would like you to go to Germany and see what more you can find out. As I said before, if you don't get any more information than what you have now, I'll close this investigation."

Louis was not sure if Jenna was telling him to continue his search because she felt guilty about taking up his time, or if she was serious about him continuing with the investigation. "Are you absolutely sure, Jenna?" he asked interrogatively. "I need to know for sure that's what you want me to do."

"Yes. I'm sure," Jenna said, feeling irritated about the way he was asking. "If you find that you're not making any progress within a month, then I'll be done with it once and for all. I promise."

"OK. Then I'll make arrangements to get on the first available flight to Germany. There's another fellow I know that would consider keeping an eye out on things for you. I'll call him to set it up," Louis said.

On that note, Louis left. He wanted to make sure Jenna was safe; that was his priority. Shaking his head, he thought, *this woman is giving me a migraine.* Not wasting any time, he immediately called the man who agreed to do the stakeout.

Louis suddenly came to the realization that he was beginning to have strong feelings for Jenna. However, that would be against his work ethic, and he had to get his mind back on track to what he had originally set out to do; it was neither the time nor the place for these feelings to emerge.

Louis rang his agent, Paul. "Hi, Paul. It's Louis. Are you still willing to keep watch for my client for the next week or so?"

"Yep. It might be for only a week. I'll let you know if I'm able to do any longer. I have another post coming up, but I'm not exactly sure when that's supposed to start."

"OK. That's not a problem. So, when can you start?" Louis asked.

"The day after tomorrow."

"Great. I'll call my client and let her know that by Friday you'll be there."

"Sounds good. Have a good trip to Germany, Louis."

"I sure would like to get this situation over with while I'm there."

"Good luck. We'll talk when you get back," Paul said and hung up.

CHAPTER TWENTY-FOUR

By Thursday, Louis's flight was booked for Hamburg, Germany, and Paul the security agent was ready to start his stakeout the following morning. Louis was eager to get this bizarre case solved, or if not completely solved, then to at least obtain enough new data to give Jenna some mental peace. He had dealt with a few difficult situations in the past, but this one topped them all. In some way, the challenge excited him. Nevertheless, the situation was still worrisome. It was essential for him obtain more significant information to help him solve this peculiar set of circumstances.

Louis did some research on the Internet about the city of Hamburg. He wanted to familiarize himself with the area before he set out.

*Hamburg is the second biggest city in Germany next to Berlin. The city has beautiful architecture and lovely scenery, with breathtaking mountains as a backdrop in some areas. The population is around 1.7 million people. There are many rural areas surrounding Hamburg. Germany has three airports: Finkenwerder, Lubeck, and the Hamburg airport. Many people from all over the globe fly in and out of these airports, seemingly undetected. If anyone wanted to set up a covert organization, it could be easily accommodated without too many questions being asked from the authorities or from those who lived around the vicinities of Hamburg or the smaller areas of Germany. And unless there were unusual occurrences, no one would bother the company or question what they were doing.[*]

---

[*] Wikipedia encyclopedia research

Louis's plane landed in Hamburg that evening. As soon as he arrived at the hotel, he went straight to his room and took out his recorder, noting his first procedure, which was to call some of his contacts. He would have to wait until morning before getting in touch with the people he knew.

He decided to go to a bar and have a drink or two before calling it a night. His mind raced with the information he had gained so far, and he thought about Jenna. *If only I'd met Jenna under different circumstances, it might have been different for both of us. But it didn't happen that way, and there's no point in stewing about it.*

As soon as daylight came through the window the next morning, Louis was up and ready for the day. After quickly showering and shaving, he put on a grey pin-stripe suit, which further elongated his six-foot-two height. Making a good impression was important, no matter who he interacted with.

He needed to arrange a meeting with the person who would provide him the other details that he didn't have. He decided to do some work on his computer while having coffee, so he sat in a quiet café that only had a few patrons. He wrote a few e-mails, and after pressing send, he started making phone calls. His first call was to the man who worked as an undercover agent in Germany.

"Hello, my name is Louis Chambeaux. I'm a detective from Paris, France. May I speak with Gunter Bergman, please?"

"Ja, Danke minute bitte." Louis was put on hold for a moment, and then another voice came on the phone. "Helloo. . . this is Gunter."

"Hello, Gunter. It's Detective Louis Chambeaux from Paris, France. A mutual colleague of ours gave me your name and number. I'm investigating a mysterious case regarding two men who lived in Alberta, Canada. One died mysteriously, and the other disappeared unexpectedly. My client was previously married to both men. I'm here in Hamburg hoping to find out whether, in some way, they were both involved with the organization that I've been told is being scrutinized by some undercover agents from Amsterdam. I know that similar events such as what my client has experienced have occurred, and I understand they have been occurring in different parts of Germany and the Netherlands. I have a feeling there might be a connection with these two men."

"Ah! So, you're here in Germany to try and find out if these men were involved in some way with what is happening around here."

"Yes, exactly. Could I set up an appointment with you today, if possible? It has become extremely important that I find out what these two men were up to," Louis asked emphatically.

"That would be fine. Come to my office after lunch, and we will go over the information you have already. If I can help to further your investigation, I will do my best."

"Thanks, Gunter. See you after lunch."

Louis made a few more calls after speaking to Gunter, and after searching the Internet for what he was looking for, he arranged some meetings with some others who would be a benefit to his investigation.

He had a quick bite to eat and then set out for Gunter's office. Arriving a few minutes before 1:00 PM. he looked around the neighborhood. Gunter's office was not in an upscale section. There were dilapidated-looking homes and buildings all around where his office was situated. It was in a building set back from the main traffic, basically hidden between two larger buildings. It took Louis a few minutes to find it. He wondered why an agent of Gunter's competence would have an office in an area that was so out-of-the-way.

It was Saturday and all seemed quiet. There were not many people about. *I guess some agents prefer it that way; it's just an aspect of being an undercover agent,* he thought. It took him a few minutes to find his office, and he walked in without knocking.

CHAPTER TWENTY-FIVE

As Louis walked into Gunter's office, he lightly tapped on the office door to let him know someone was there. A voice said, "Come in."

Gunter sat at his desk smoking a cigarette. He was a dishevelled looking man. His eyes looked as though they could pop from their sockets at any moment. His wrinkled shirt hung out from his trousers, and he hadn't shaven in a few days. His wide shoulders and muscular chest emphasized his unkempt appearance even more.

Bundles of folders, some documents, a tablet, and two computers filled the entire space on his desk, aside for a small area for his laptop, which he used for his most important work. Shelves around the room were crammed with books, and an ashtray beside the laptop overflowed with stale, half-smoked cigarettes butts. The office reeked of stale cigarette smoke, over-brewed coffee, and leftover food from takeout meals, and the office obviously hadn't been cleaned for some time.

Louis looked around, hesitating to sit down anywhere.

Gunter pointed to a chair away from his desk. "My cleaning lady has left me for other employment. As you can see, my office is in dire need of a good cleaning," he chuckled.

"Mmm, yes, I can see that," Louis commented, forcing a smile as he pulled up the chair.

"Here, let me clear some of this stuff off my desk first, then we'll get down to business." He picked up a bunch of folders and papers and threw them in a corner onto the floor, dumped the full ashtray in a waste paper basket, and quickly dusted the top of the desk with a cloth.

"Now, that's a bit better. Please, pull the chair up closer. Do you have data to show me, or just recordings of your finds?"

"I have both, but before we get into that, I wanted to tell you about some other things," Louis said.

Louis told Gunter the whole story about Jenna, beginning with her experiences with Gary and Brandon and what the police found when they did the searches in Alberta, and finally, he concluded with his own findings.

"It's an interesting situation you've taken on, here. There have been similar events in different locations around Germany with people who have gone missing, and there have been some mysterious deaths as well. To my knowledge, there are at least five men, in recent months, who have either mysteriously disappeared or died. The bodies of the dead men were never found. Each man apparently worked at a different job. Three of the five men were married, and their wives to this day are still devastated and mystified by their husbands' sudden disappearances."

Gunter stood up and looked out the window for a few minutes. He took two strong puffs of his cigarette before continuing their conversation. "There is definitely something very strange taking place," Gunter remarked, "but I'm unsure exactly what it all means. A couple of colleagues and I have reason to believe there is at least one organization near Hamburg, which is creating much interest among some of the secret agents. This organization is an obscure enterprise, and we think there is a connection with the missing and dead men. Chances are, there are probably other establishments like it elsewhere in the world. It may be bigger than we expect. It almost seems unworldly, if you know what I mean."

Gunter was a chain smoker, and as he butts one cigarette out he immediately lit another. He sat back in his chair, mulling over what he just said to Louis for a few seconds.

"I know exactly what you're saying," Louis said, nodding. "Here are my records. You'll note there are similarities to what you have just told me. I also suspected that there might be more to these unusual occurrences. What else do we need to do to uncover what this organization is doing?"

Gunter looked over the information Louis had gathered on Brandon and Gary. "You have gathered a good amount of information, but we need more proof to get to the real reason behind these mysterious events. It's a catch-22, I must admit. I'm preparing a meeting with some agents from another secret service agency from outside of Hamburg. These agents will be providing more facts."

"Yes, there needs to be more evidence, something that will bring us closer to what's behind these mysterious deaths and disappearances," Louis agreed, and he loosened his tie. It was getting stuffy in Gunter's office with all the smoke residue building up.

"We will be very busy for the next few weeks or more. There's a big meeting scheduled for next Tuesday at a gymnasium not far from here." Gunter tore a piece of scrap paper, scribbled the address on it, and gave it to Louis. "Here is the address. We're looking at spending the day going over all the data that we have on hand and perhaps coming up with a greater plan to catch whoever is responsible for all these strange actions. It's our hope that we can apprehend them before anything else happens."

"I'm curious about something," Louis interjected." Do you know if any of the men in the organization you mentioned wear black one-piece uniform style outfits?"

"It's interesting you should ask that," Gunter replied, looking intently at Louis. "Yes. I was informed of this peculiar dress code. Why do you ask? Were the men who followed your client dressed in the same manner?"

"The exact same style," Louis said.

Gunter grunted. "Mmm, there is definitely something brewing," he remarked.

"I wonder how many more of these characters are out there, and where are they situated," Louis asked, wanting to know more.

"That's a question a few people are asking. I think we're in for an interesting ride," Gunter added.

"It sure sounds like it. I'm staying at the Heidelberg Hotel if you need to reach me."

Gunter butt out his cigarette, walked to the filthy window, and stood there again, looking out for a couple of minutes before saying anything else. He turned to Louis, his brow wrinkling. "It's not going to be an easy task by any means, but maybe if there are enough of us working on this situation, we'll be able to put a stop to whatever these men are attempting to do."

"God! I sure hope so. Alright, I'll see you on Tuesday," Louis said as he got up to leave.

"Tuesday, it is," Gunter nodded.

"Oh, I meant to ask you, is there a nice restaurant around here that you recommend? And a bar, so I can have a couple of drinks before I try to get some sleep? I'm not sure I will sleep, but maybe with a couple . . ."

"I know only too well what you're saying," Gunter responded and gave him the names of a good restaurant and a bar. "Try and rest if you can. You will need to be sharp as a razor for the upcoming weeks."

"I'll try. Good night." Louis left feeling perplexed by all the events that had occurred in different parts of Europe and in Canada.

"Night," Gunter replied.

CHAPTER TWENTY-SIX

Louis felt like he needed to have a couple of beers before returning to his hotel room. Sitting at the bar that Gunter had suggested was quite interesting. There were some odd-looking characters talking to one another. They appeared as though they might be of the type that he and Gunter had spoken about, but then he thought, *No, surely, they wouldn't be out in public like this.* After he finished one last beer, he set out to his room.

Being in his room would give him an opportunity to delve further into the investigation a little more, regarding the information some of the agents have found out, before the meeting takes place at the gymnasium that Gunter mentioned

He spent Sunday and Monday making calls, and talking to some officials who were in a higher government capacity. He received basically the same information from the government officials that Gunter had given him. Still having some extra time on his hands, he made a call to Jenna and

Andrea. He wanted to keep them up to date on the status of the investigation as much as possible.

"Hi, Jenna. How are things going? Anything going on lately that I should know about?"

"Hi, Louis. No, there's been nothing out of the ordinary lately, thank goodness. Andrea and I have been staying in a lot. How is your search going in Germany?"

"That's what I'm calling you about. I spoke to a secret service agent yesterday, and he told me some very interesting things. There's an organization near Hamburg that the agency is watching. This organization apparently keeps a very low profile, and it might be a key factor in this investigation. There have also been a few strange deaths and disappearances in some other areas of Germany and the Netherlands." Louis paused for a moment and then continued. "I was also informed that Brandon was the leader of this nefarious organization. I'm going to an important meeting in a few days with an agent named Gunter and some other agents to discuss what steps are needed to catch whoever is responsible for these ongoing disappearances and deaths."

Jenna was astounded. "Oh, Wow! Brandon was their leader. The more you tell me about Brandon, the more I realize how utterly clueless I was about him. It sounds like you're making headway."

"Yes, but I should know even more after I attend the meeting next Tuesday. At least now I know there's something going on around different parts of the globe. I'll call you sometime after the meeting."

"OK, Louis, keep me in the loop of things," Jenna said, and they both hung up.

* * *

Louis went through all his records again, thinking maybe he would notice something that he hadn't seen before, but nothing popped out at him.

Getting increasingly anxious, he wanted to move on with the present state of affairs. By Monday, he couldn't stand it any longer and called Gunter to see if there was anything else he should know. "Hi, Gunter. Do you have any more information for me since we last spoke?"

"No, nothing, but the meeting is on tomorrow," Gunter replied.

"I want to get on with it. I'm having a difficult time sitting around when I know there are things that need to be done."

"One step at a time, Louis. It will get done. How about you meet me here at 9:00 AM? We'll go together to the meeting at the gymnasium," Gunter said.

"I'll be there."

● * *

The next morning, Louis was up and ready earlier than usual. He stopped at a bistro and picked up a coffee, then set out for Gunter's office.

Gunter was slamming his paper holder on the desk and tossing folders on the floor as Louis walked into his office.

"Not in a good mood today, I see," Louis said. "What's going on?"

"I just got a call about the meeting. It seems that there are restrictions being put forth regarding some of the procedures we want to implement. I didn't get all the details, but it doesn't sound good for us."

"What do you mean, what kind of restrictions?" Louis asked.

"There are some people involved with these investigations who are opposing certain steps that we want to do to find out what these evil bozos are up to, like twenty-four-hour surveillance and phone tapping."

"Do you plan to go ahead with what we need to do, even with these people issuing limitations?" Louis asked.

"These so called know-it-all types of people infuriate me. Well you know what, fuck them, we have to do what we need to do," Gunter said.

"Let's go listen to what these concerns are before you get more riled up," Louis replied.

The meeting was being held at a gymnasium because of the large sum of people attending. The issue about the organization Nebula's Moon was a serious one for many, it seemed. However, there were still some people, like corporation lawyers, government officials, and business owners of Germany and Amsterdam, who felt otherwise.

Louis watched the people as they entered the sports building. There were a lot who attended—some women, but mostly men. As Louis gazed around the room, he noticed one man standing by the door who didn't seem to fit in with the rest of the crowd. He was an older man with an outlandish spiked haircut and dressed all in black. His expression seemed frozen.

Louis moved toward Gunter to point the man out to him, but the man was no longer standing there by the time he approached Gunter.

"Gunter, I just saw a strange looking man standing over by the doorway. He didn't seem to fit in with the rest of the crowd here. He was just here, all of two minutes ago, but now he's gone. I think this person might be a spy."

"What makes you say that? What appeared to be strange about him?" Gunter asked.

Louis told him about the way he looked. "My gut feeling tells me there's something different about this man, Gunter. I think he might mean trouble."

Gunter raised an eyebrow. "We shouldn't judge every odd-looking fellow that comes in here. But if you really think it might be a serious matter, then keep an eye out for him. If he returns, let me know, and I'll consider it," Gunter said, and the two men returned to their seats.

An officious looking man stepped up onto to the platform and introduced himself. "Hello everyone. My name is Karl Vanderwaltz, and I am the Chief Agent of one of Germany's secret agencies. I want to thank you all for attending this meeting."

Vanderwaltz began to speak about the strange events that had been occurring for the past year in certain regions of Germany and the Netherlands. He emphasized that these circumstances involved mysterious disappearances and, in some instances, unexplained deaths. He went on to say that he and his colleagues had compiled a batch of information, which they received from some undisclosed witnesses in regards to some of these incidences and which indicated that an organizational involvement was at hand.

Two other agents in the audience were invited up to talk about what they had found during their investigations and what they thought needed to be accomplished to catch the individuals involved in these strange events.

As the two agents spoke, Louis continued to scrutinize the audience to see if he could spot the strange man from before, but he didn't see him amongst the crowd.

A few people who opposed certain steps that would be taken to catch the perpetrators spoke up. They argued that it was not necessary to have a twenty-four-hour surveillance of the building these strange men were reportedly occupying.

This was then refuted by those who wanted the unexplained actions permanently stopped; one way for that to happen, they argued, would be to have some agents enter a premise or building without a search warrant if it was deemed crucial enough to do so, and to do phone tapping. However, those procedures violated certain statutes and laws of some of the areas involved.

Toward the end of the meeting, it was decided that the only way to come to a final decision was to take a vote of all attendees who were for or against the proposed procedures. The result of the vote indicated a strong agreement to place all measures in operation to cease the harmful activities that had been taking place.

The meeting ended, but not without some volatile discussions first. Gunter was livid with those who opposed the proposed methods. He made a valid point about some of the men who died. "The deaths of these men were never clearly substantiated. There are people out there that are responsible for these despicable acts, and they need to be brought to justice!" he said loudly so that everyone in the gymnasium could hear him. Gunter ended his outburst when he saw the man that Louis had mentioned briefly dash in and out again.

Louis rushed over to Gunter. "Gunter, that same man was here again. I saw him come in, and then quickly leave again. I think he's observing what we're doing here. Why else would he be here for the second time and leave so fast? There's a good possibility that this person may have been sent to this meeting to hear about our plans. Damn, we never thought to ask for any identification?" Louis said. His expression indicated that he was extremely concerned about this man's brief presence, and he realized they had overlooked the matter of asking for proof of identity. In that case, how many others were there here, spying on them?

"I know, I saw him this time," Gunter said heatedly. "You could be on the money with this guy. I'll mention it to the head spokesperson." He swiftly marched over to speak to the head spokesperson.

Gunter was quick to approach the leader to inform him of what he and Louis had observed and that he was extremely concerned that they were being spied on. The leader immediately gathered those who were an integral part of the meeting and conveyed what Gunter had told him.

The group decided to take immediate steps to ascertain who this person was. It spurred a lot of commotion, with voices blaring and people running about searching for the anonymous character. No one else had paid any attention to the mysterious man, and those men who searched for him had been unable to discover who this person was by the time the meeting ended. But it was decided that a few agents and police officers would be looking further into the matter.

Gunter and Louis stopped for a quick beer before Gunter went back to his office. They wanted to talk about the man they saw at the meeting. Both men came to the same conclusion: it had to be someone from the secret organization, Nebula's Moon, spying on them. They made up their minds to make their own inquiries and to start the next day.

CHAPTER TWENTY-SEVEN

Jenna and Andrea, in the meantime, were tired of staying indoors and called the new agent Paul to let him know they would be going out. It would probably be Andrea's last good meal and night out in Paris, and they wanted to make a special evening of it.

"Hi Paul, this is Jenna. Louis told me that you are our new stakeout agent. Andrea and I would like to have a night out. It's been a while since we last stepped away from our room. Are you fine with doing the watch tonight?"

"Not a problem, Jenna. I won't be too far behind you. What time are you heading out?"

"We've made dinner reservations for 7:00 at the Chateaux. I'll inform the supervisor that we will be out having dinner."

"Alright, then I won't be far away."

"Thank you," Jenna replied.

They women excitedly chatted while preparing for their evening. It seemed like such a long time since they had been away from the four walls of their room they had become accustomed to. It was comforting to know that another agent would be looking after their safety while they were out for the evening.

The Chateaux turned out to be an excellent choice of restaurant. The décor was superb, with the Victorian art displays and ornate fixtures and furniture. It felt like they were being transported back in time to the Victorian period.

Deciding this was a special occasion, Jenna and Andrea decided to splurge and ordered an expensive red wine to have with their meal, which consisted of a shrimp dish and a mixed salad with pears and almonds, tossed with the restaurant's famous house dressing.

While they waited for their dinner, they joked with each other, laughing to the point of tears. Jenna couldn't remember the last time she had laughed so much. It felt good not to worry about her state of affairs for a change.

As the women enjoyed their dinner, Paul stood just outside the restaurant beside the doorway, watching for anything that appeared to be unusual. He spotted a figure in a laneway across the road. At first, the person didn't appear to be out of the ordinary, but as he continued to examine the individual, he noticed another man wearing the same style of black clothing approaching the first man. He assumed they were members of a religious cult or something of that nature. He didn't want them to see him watching and stood further back in the doorway.

As he started to retreat, the two men bolted like lighting across the road. One of the men held what looked like a laser type of weapon. Paul couldn't tell what it was exactly.

When they came toward him, Paul pulled out his gun, readying for an assault. Suddenly, a bright ray of light ejected from the strange projectile and hit him in the chest. Though he was a strong man, the beam caused him to tumble to the ground, paralyzed. He couldn't move his legs. As he laid there, the strange men came nearer to him and said, *"We are not here to cause harm, we have only a mission to fulfill. Cease these observations or harm will be the outcome."* Within seconds, they completely vanished from his sight.

Paul was stupefied. In all his years working as an agent, he had never encountered anything like it. His legs regained mobility after about fifteen minutes, and he resolved that it was vital to call Louis and tell him what had just occurred.

As he struggled to manoeuvre his legs, he clutched his cell phone to call Louis. He got only Louis's voice mail in answer. "Louis, it's Paul. Call me as soon as possible. It's really urgent."

The incident unnerved him, but the only thing for him to do at that point was to contact his immediate supervisor to tell him about his experience. His car was parked close by, and even though his legs still felt wobbly, he could drive. He wasted no time in getting to the office. He suddenly realized that he had left the women unprotected and immediately called Jenna on her cell phone. They were still in the restaurant when he called.

Jenna and Andrea were just about ready to leave the restaurant when Jenna heard her phone ringing.

"Hi, Jenna speaking."

Paul, still shaken, blurted out what had happened to him and told them to get in a cab and get back to the centre right away. It was important that he speak with his supervisor about this episode. He was on his way there now, and he'd call them later.

Jenna sat back down, unable to say anything. "What was that all about?" Andrea asked with concern in her voice.

Jenna stammered as she attempted to tell Andrea what Paul had told her.

"Get a grip, what's the problem? Tell me!" Andrea asked, not understanding Jenna's reaction.

"Paul . . ." Jenna said, trying to keep calm, "was just attacked by two men dressed in black. They were carrying a weapon of some sort, and he was immobilized for a while. He said we should get to the centre right away. He'll get in touch with us later."

"What! I can't believe this is happening again. Let's get our butts there, now." The women were quick to get their coats on and pay the bill. Hurrying out of the restaurant, they got into a cab that was parked on the street. Frightened, Andrea said to the cab driver, "Hurry, take us to the women's centre."

"What's the matter, lady? You seem really upset. Is there anything that I can do for you?"

"It's too complicated to explain. We just need to get to the centre as fast as possible," Jenna replied, with a shaky voice.

"Not a problem." The cab driver drove as fast as he could, sensing they were in a troubled state.

CHAPTER TWENTY-EIGHT

Paul dashed into the agency office. "Is Ivan in? I need to speak with him, it's important."

"I'll see how busy he is. One moment," the secretary said.

"Ivan, Paul is here and wants to speak with you. It sounds important."

"Tell him to come in."

Ivan was busy working on another case when Paul barged into his office. "Ivan, I know you're busy, but something of a serious nature happened to me a little while ago. I have a feeling it has to do with the investigations that are being done on these mysterious events that keep happening." He continued to tell Ivan all the details about what happened to him outside of the restaurant.

"I'll get on this right away," Ivan said genuinely concerned after Paul finished telling him what happened.

"We'll need more help than we currently have with finding these characters. I'll get a couple of men from one of the special units to consider this situation." Ivan always tried to remain calm and poised when circumstances like this occurred, but deep within he felt alarmed by this episode.

"The sooner the better. I've put a call through to Louis on his voice mail, telling him it was important for him to call me as soon as possible."

"OK, Paul, leave it with me. As soon as I get this arranged, I'll have my troop scout that whole area where you were. Maybe they will come across something."

"Speak with you later. I'll try Louis again."

Paul dialed Louis's cell phone number. Louis answered the call this time.

"Hi, this is Louis."

"It's Paul. There was an attack made on me a few hours just past while I was doing a stakeout for Jenna and Andrea.

Two men dressed in strange black clothes were skulking around a building across from the restaurant where Jenna and Andrea were having dinner. At first, I thought they were members of a cult of some type. I didn't want them to see me, so I backed off and waited to see what they were going to do. Suddenly, a beam shot forth from some type of weapon they carried. It paralyzed me for a time. They came closer to me and one of them said, 'We are not here to cause anyone harm. We have only a mission to fulfill. Cease these observations or harm will be the outcome.' And then, with a flick of a finger, they disappeared. It was really bizarre."

"That is a threat," Louis replied, alarmed. Are you OK?'

"I was shaken up for a bit, but I'm fine now. I spoke to Ivan and told him what happened, and he's considering getting a couple of the guys from the special police unit on it."

"From the sound of things, it's necessary. I still have a couple of things to do here in Hamburg before I head back to

Paris. As soon as I'm done, I'll be there. In the meantime, keep me in the loop about anything else that arises. How are the women? Do they know what happened?" Louis asked, fearing the worst.

"Yes. I thought they should know. I told them to get to the centre right away. They were pretty shaken when I told them."

"This situation is becoming much more critical. We no longer have a choice but to get a swat team to assist. Keep checking up on the women. I'm glad you're OK," Louis added.

"I will. Thanks. Talk to you later." Paul hung up feeling very uneasy about the present state of affairs

Louis was bowled over by the news. It had become even more crucial for him to wind up his affairs in Germany and get back to Paris. Through all the new contacts that he made, he had uncovered that Brandon was not transparent about his affairs on any level and that he hadn't spoken about his past to anyone. Louis thought that said a lot about him. It seemed odd from the onset of Jenna's description of him that he never spoke about his family. Louis had no doubt in his mind that he was a part of the organization that the agents were investigating. Brandon did work for a time for a legal department doing some research, and he also worked for the economics department in Alberta under a different last name, but that was all Louis had been able to learn about him. He called Gunter to let him know that he would be leaving soon for Paris because of the growing problematic situation.

"OK, Louis. I will look after things here in the meantime. I hope it all gets resolved soon for your client's sake."

"Yeah, so I do I. I'll be in touch when I know more. I'm flying out tomorrow morning."

"Good luck Louis. We'll talk soon."

After hanging up the phone, Louis packed his belongings, but he kept out his recorder in case he found a need for it. A flight was available early the next morning; it was a lucky break to have found one available so soon. He was edgy and decided to have a bite to eat at one of the pubs near the hotel. His cell phone rang while he was sitting at the bar. It was Jenna.

"Hi. Louis. Paul told us about the attack that was made on him. Andrea is going back to Alberta in a couple of days, and I've decided to go back with her. I'm too terrified of being alone in Paris, especially now, after this second attack. I think I'll stay with her for a while. Until this matter is solved, I don't think Paris is a safe place for me to be alone."

"Oh!" Louis exclaimed, surprised at the news. "I was on my way back to Paris tomorrow. If you're heading home, then there's no point in my being there."

"I'm sorry, Louis. I would feel a lot more comfortable being home with people I know."

"I totally understand, Jenna. Then, I think I will change my plans and stay in Germany to do more investigating. Things are in the works as we speak. A special police team is being organized right now to search for the offenders."

"Great. I sure hope they find whoever it is that are doing these things." Jenna sighed. She felt a little safer knowing she would be back in Alberta soon, though.

"Yeah, same here. OK, take care. I'll call you in about a week. That should give you some time to settle down."

"Alright, Louis. Good luck with everything." Jenna was disappointed about not being able to continue to stay in Paris, but she also knew it was for the best until the situation at hand gets solved.

Once Jenna had spoken to Louis, Jenna and Andrea made plans to fly out early afternoon on the following

Monday. Jenna anxiously wanted to be with the people she knew best back home. Andrea was glad that Jenna had made up her mind up to go back to Alberta with her. The experience in Paris had been horrifying, and Jenna needed some respite from it all.

CHAPTER TWENTY-NINE

When the flight landed in Alberta, Jenna felt a great sense of relief; she could feel the tension flowing away from her neck and shoulders. It was cold, though, and the snow was heavily piled everywhere—the weather was an aspect of living in Alberta that she was less than keen about. Tired and frustrated with everything, she wanted some peace away from whoever had been following her and initiating those terrible attacks. As far as getting her old job back, she decided she wasn't quite ready to go back to work, at least not for a while.

Andrea suggested that Jenna could stay at her place for if she liked. Even she felt exhausted from the experience in Paris. It was a puzzling set of circumstances, and she hoped that they wouldn't have to deal with those characters who had followed them in Paris anymore, now that they were back home in Alberta.

The apartment building where Andrea lived was in a quieter area of Prince George. It backed onto a lovely golf course, which overflowed with geese and ducks in the late summer. Deer sometimes made an entrance, and moose would make an appearance occasionally, too. She loved her place. It was peaceful and quiet; in her opinion, it was a great place for Jenna to gain back her strength and enjoy some peaceful moments. Although it was only a one bedroom apartment, Andrea had a pull-out sofa bed, and there was plenty of room for both. It would be perfect for them to live comfortably for a short time.

It took them an hour and a half to get to Andrea's apartment complex from the airport. Neither spoke during the ride in the airport shuttle. Jenna gazed out the car window, looking at the snow-covered ground and highways. The hydro lines were coated with thick ice, and frozen ponds glistened like iced popsicles. Alberta was a big province, and new developments were constantly being established with highways being extended and construction projects being put into operation.

Jenna was disappointed she couldn't have stayed in Paris for longer, but if those frightening series of events continued, she felt safer being in Alberta. Paris was a beautiful city, but unfortunately, it hadn't been a pleasant visit.

Finally, the women arrived at Andrea's apartment. Both took deep breaths as they entered the apartment.

"Whew, I'm so glad to be back in my own place. It's too bad things were the way they were in Paris. Perhaps sometime down the line, when all is solved, I'll travel there again," Andrea said.

"I'm so sorry that it didn't turn out to be an enjoyable trip for you, Andrea. I sure didn't expect it to be that way."

"I know you didn't. But now that we're here, let's enjoy it. Maybe we could make some plans to go on a few weekend trips while you're staying here," Andrea said. She looked at Jenna to see how she would react.

"I'm up for that, anything to take my mind from the past couple of months," Jenna replied, feeling hopeful. She plopped herself down on Andrea's sofa as though she hadn't sat on a comfortable sofa in a long time.

Andrea pulled the drapes open and noticed that the sun was setting. It was a magnificent sunset with an array of pinkish and purple colours saturating the sky. It felt magical and was pleasantly welcome after their terrifying experience in Paris.

After unpacking their luggage, they decided to order in. Both were weary, and ordering something in was ideal at that point. Neither of them felt like cooking.

The apartment was warm and cozy. A bright, colourful chesterfield and matching loveseat filled the centre of the living room in front of the bay window, which overlooked the golf course. The décor was a cross selection of modern-day and antique pieces, accentuated with silk flower arrangements, contemporary figurines, and ornamental wall sconces.

"You did a beautiful job with this place, Andrea. I love how you've arranged things in here," Jenna commented, impressed by Andrea's decorative flair.

"Thanks, it's comfortable. I have some wine; would you like to have a glass before we call it a night?"

"Sure, that would be nice," Jenna said, sighing with sense of relief.

Andrea inserted a disk in her CD player, and soft classical music began to play. She opened a bottle of red wine and filled two glasses. Sighing deeply, they sat down with their wine. Andrea flicked the TV on, checking what programs were playing. It had been a while since they last watched television for any length of time.

Jenna suddenly noticed that music was playing and the television was on at the same time. "Andrea, aren't we wanting quiet for a while?" Jenna asked. "You have music playing and the television on."

Andrea turned to look at Jenna, totally caught in the moment. She immediately shut the TV off. "You're right. Let's just sit and listen to the soft music and talk."

"I wonder how Louis is making out in Germany," Jenna pondered out loud.

"Maybe you should call him later this week and see if there's been any progress," Andrea suggested.

"Yeah, I think I will," Jenna responded.

CHAPTER THIRTY

Since he wasn't going to Paris, Louis arranged to stay in Germany to continue with his investigation. He understood why Jenna needed to be home, and he didn't blame her. The situation at hand was unpredictable as things currently stood. The first thing he wanted to do was call Gunter to let him know he wouldn't be flying back to Paris and that he would be staying in Germany a while longer.

"Hello, Gunter. It's Louis. There's been a change of plans. I won't be going back to Paris after all. My client has decided to go back to Alberta. I would like to get together with you and discuss the next steps we should be looking at taking. I don't know if you're aware of the incident that happened to Paul, one of Paris's agent—an attack was made on him just the other night. This is clearly the result of an organized effort, and we have to find out who's directing these actions."

"Fucking bastards!" Gunter swore. "Not another one. I'll be available later today. How about we get a late lunch and we can go over things while we eat?"

"Great. Around 2:00?"

"Sounds good. Meet me at the last place we had lunch," Gunter replied.

"OK, see you then."

After Louis hung up, he went through all the data he had compiled so that he and Gunter could go over things in an orderly fashion.

The men met at the stipulated time and place, ordered lunch, and began discussing the potential dangers that would be involved if they continued to unravel the workings of the Nebula's Moon. They both agreed that the organization was a big part of the ongoing events.

"I suggest that you keep checking into the matter with Brandon Styles," Gunter said with a serious countenance. "It sounds as though this man was an integral part of this surreptitious establishment."

"I agree. From what Jenna told me about him, he was obviously hiding a lot of things from her. He never talked about his past, and his disappearance was very puzzling for those who investigated the circumstances," Louis said as he stroked his brow.

They spent the greater part of the afternoon going over more details, talking about the events that took place recently, and they tossed around what might be at the heart of the matter at hand. They both felt the organization wanted control over the people living on earth, perhaps for purposes of propagating their own kind; that was an aspect that needed to be answered.

Gunter's phone rang as they were talking. "Hello, this is Gunter."

"Gunter, it's Ivan." Ivan was the Chief Inspector for one of the police departments in Germany. "Can you come to my office as soon as possible? The special investigation team came across something that I think will be of great interest to you."

"Louis and I are just finishing up with something. We will both be there shortly."

As he hung up, the look in his eyes told Louis that something critical was up.

"I gather we need to get to Ivan's office immediately," Louis commented.

"Ja, sounds serious."

While Louis and Gunter were setting out for Ivan's office, Ivan requested that the special unit attend as well.

Louis and Gunter were quick in getting to the office. The special team was already there, waiting to disclose what they found.

Ivan spoke first. "I have asked you to be here this morning to inform you about what the team has come across, and Martin will be speaking about this."

The head of the investigation bureau then spoke. "Good morning, everyone. My name is Martin, and I'm in charge of the special investigation unit of this area. As you know, strange events have been occurring over the past year throughout Germany, the Netherlands, and other parts of the world as well.

"We received an anonymous tip regarding some activities going on in an abandoned building located on the outskirts of Hamburg near Barsbutte. When we went into the building, we found strange pieces of technology, unknown to this side of the globe. This technology is constructed with some type of material that no one here has any knowledge about. As far as we are aware, it's not something that was developed here in Germany, and we have reason to believe there are people—or perhaps, I should say, entities—looking to make changes in different parts of the world for purposes yet unknown to us."

"How did you conclude that it's not made here in Germany?" Louis asked.

"The technology was examined by a couple of our expert materials engineers, who have extensive knowledge about different types of materials, and they were unable to determine what it was. They have deduced that the type of substance used is unknown to our world, as far as they are able to determine," Martin continued to state. He was a tall man with wide shoulders, which make him appear intimidating.

"What you're saying is that the earth is being visited by beings from another planet?" Ivan asked with skepticism.

"Yes," Martin replied with certainty. "We think that there are beings from another galaxy here on earth wanting to make changes to our planet. What these changes are—well, that is what we're trying to ascertain."

"What more is needed to find who, or whatever it is, that's trying to expedite these changes?" Gunter then asked, not believing what he was hearing.

"We won't be able to do too much more at this point, until such a time that another attempt is made to harm or kill someone," Martin replied.

"What do you mean? Why do we have to wait until someone else dies or is harmed before something is done?" Louis asked tersely.

"At this point in time, we have no other choice," Martin sternly countered. "We also found what appears to be a form of communication, a series of cryptograms jotted down on a sheet of old parchment paper. We think they were left behind on purpose. What these codes mean, we haven't been able to decipher yet; we are working on it. They may provide a clue to who these beings are or what they are planning on doing."

Everyone in the room was astounded at what they heard. They all looked at each other, not knowing what else to ask or add to Martin's disclosure.

Martin continued, "The special unit will continue to monitor the situation very closely. Whoever these beings are, they will more than likely set up somewhere else, now. No doubt they know that we've been to this building."

Even though Ivan had an idea of what Martin would be saying at the meeting, Ivan then spoke. "In the interim, we all need to keep a tight vigilance on any unusual incidences. Please inform Martin of anything that may be suspicious. Until such time that there is another attempt made to harm or kill someone, we have no recourse in the matter. Let's keep on with our efforts to find out what they're planning on."

"Gentlemen," Martin continued, "that is all I have to say for today. Carry on with what you were doing, and perhaps with time, greater evidence will become available. Please, keep your eyes open and your ears peeled for anything that may seem out of the ordinary" he concluded.

Ivan turned to Louis. "In the meantime, I suggest that you carry on with what you were working on. Who knows what else it might reveal?"

"If nothing else comes from my investigation, I hope to at least find out who or what is responsible for these attacks," Louis said. "I'm curious."

All the men wore concerned expressions on their faces as they walked out of the meeting. Louis felt wary. *What's it going to mean for everyone and for Jenna?* he wondered. Some strange characters had been pursuing her, and the reason was still unknown.

After the rest of the men left, Gunter, Ivan, and Louis decided to continue their conversation at a local tavern. Gunter and Louis were alarmed by the information they had learned at the meeting.

CHAPTER THIRTY-ONE

At the tavern, the three men ordered a large pitcher of beer. As they filled their glasses, they began discussing.

"That was certainly an interesting meeting. What did you both think about what Martin said?" Ivan asked.

"Well, we now know that there's definitely something going on, and that it'll require all the attention possible," Gunter responded.

"I got the feeling there was more information available than what Martin was prepared to give us. I don't think Martin wanted to share everything he knew, for some reason," Louis commented.

"Well, I do know that the special unit is under strict orders, depending on the matter at hand, to keep some of their information between themselves and Martin for security reasons," Ivan stated. "What are you going to say to the two women? Will you tell them everything we heard today?" he asked Louis.

"No. I think I will hold off on telling them everything. Jenna, especially, has been through a lot already. I'm not sure at this point how much of it I should tell her and her friend, Andrea. I think it might put Jenna over the edge."

"Personally, I think the less you say, the better. Why should you upset them any more than they are already? It's up to us, Martin, and the special teams to get this solved," Gunter emphatically commented.

"You're absolutely right," Ivan replied.

The three men sat for a little while longer, then thought it best to get a move on with the affairs. They each had their own agendas to look after regarding the strange events.

"Alright. I need to get back to my office. Let's keep in touch with one another to stay abreast of things. Maybe with luck, this will be over in the not-too-distant future. I'll give you a call in a couple of days to check in on things. In the meantime, do whatever you can," Ivan said as he got up to leave. Ivan appeared confident, but he never let on that he felt uneasy and uncertain about how it would all work out for everyone concerned.

"We will keep you informed, you can be sure of that," Gunter said, and Louis nodded in agreement. They looked at one another with perplexed expressions before walking off.

"OK. I plan on getting started as soon as I get to my place," Louis said to Gunter, getting up to leave as well. "Good luck with your efforts, Gunter. I hope I can obtain more knowledge," he said, finishing their conversation.

"You and me both. We'll talk soon," Gunter replied. He and Louis left the tavern and went in different directions.

Louis sat in his car for a few minutes before driving off toward his hotel. Trying to figure out what these beings were organizing mentally exhausted him. It was extremely important to crack open this case once and for all. Nonetheless, that would mean working long hours, and lots of reports remained to be written.

He drove as fast as he could to the hotel. Not paying proper attention, he almost sideswiped another car. He realized then how tense he had become. He needed to ease up.

When he attempted to slow down, he noticed a car tailgating him in his rear-view mirror. He honked his horn, but the driver ignored it and drove up even closer, crashing against the back bumper of Louis's car. Louis quickly pulled over to the side of the road and jumped out to confront the driver, but when he stepped out in front of the car to stop the individual, Louis was nearly run over. The driver rapidly wheeled his car around and drove in the other direction.

Louis shuddered down to his bones. It took him a few minutes to calm down. Grasping his cell phone, he immediately called Gunter. "Gunter, someone tried to run me down just now. I didn't get a good look at the driver—the car windows were tinted. Someone is trying to kill me. Son-of-a-bitch. I think we may have shaken things up a bit, from the sounds of it," Louis said, clearly upset.

"Ja, I think so, too. I suggest you get to another hotel as soon as possible for your own safety. Keep a close eye out, and carry a gun with you. Call me when you get there."

"Got you," Louis said. His hand shook as he hung up.

Louis wasted no time getting to his current hotel to pick up his things. When he opened the door, he saw that the room had been ransacked. *Thank goodness, I had all my records with me,* he thought.

Hurrying as fast as he could to get away from the hotel, he paid the clerk and told her he wouldn't be back. He decided to get a room at a hotel further away before calling Gunter. He scanned the area before getting into his car, making sure no one was following him before he left. Nothing seemed suspicious as he drove away.

As he drove along, the bright lights of the city somehow seemed liked they were dimming off and on, and it felt to him that the traffic around him heralded greater carefulness.

Rubbing the back of his neck to release the building tension, Louis thought about the continual rise of events. As a detective, sometimes stressful circumstances came with the territory, but this particular situation brought much more danger and stress than he had expected. His thoughts were frenzied. *This whole affair must be solved soon. I don't know how much more I can handle.*

Louis found a hotel further away from the busiest part of Hamburg. As he checked in, he gazed around the hotel lobby. He didn't see anyone suspicious about. Regardless, he knew that it was important for him to take greater precaution. As soon as he got to his room, he called Gunter.

"Gunter, when I got back to my hotel room, someone had already been there and ransacked the room. I'm glad I was carrying all my records with me at the time."

"It could be the same person who tried to run you down earlier. It's come to the point that we need to get all special police units on hand, immediately. Get yourself to another hotel as soon as possible."

"I've done that already. I'm at the Palisade Hotel about ten miles down from the main route," Louis said.

"I know exactly where it is. Stay there. I'll get Ivan get on this right away," Gunter said with urgency in his voice.

"I don't plan on going anywhere right now, but I'll be more discreet about the inquiries I make, in the meantime."

"OK. As soon as I can get a hold of Ivan, I'll give you a ring."

"I'll be here."

CHAPTER THIRTY-TWO

The first thing Louis did after he hung up was call Jenna and Andrea. Jenna was busy making dinner when the phone rang.

"Hello?" she answered while chopping up some vegetables for soup.

"Hi, Jenna. It's Louis. How are you?"

"Hi, Louis. I'm OK. I'm making dinner now. So, what's happening? Anything new since we last spoke?"

"Yes, actually. I'm working with two undercover agents who are part of a special police team. Together we're working on a plan to uncover the activities of a secret organization near Hamburg. We think finding out about this group may be the key we need to solve the strange incidents that have been going on." Louis was very careful about how much information he divulged to Jenna, not wanting to upset her any more than she already was. "I'll call you in a week."

"Thanks for keeping in touch. I really hope they catch whoever these characters are." She hung up and passed on the information onto Andrea.

"I can't believe it's gone this far. Louis is a great detective, and if he's working with other undercover agents, it will get solved," Andrea commented after Jenna finished telling her Louis's news.

"I don't know, Andrea. I think this situation has become much more extreme than Louis ever thought it would be. It sounds to me like there's is a lot more to the story than what he's telling me."

"Hmm," Andrea paused while considering the implications. "I hope it won't continue to affect you or me any more than it has already."

It had been a couple of weeks since they last went out, and they decided to go out shopping the next day. Andrea asked a male cousin of hers to tag along with the; it would make them both feel safer. He agreed. They told him a little about what was happening, but not all the details.

Meanwhile, Louis continued his investigation. He made a call to a police department in Vancouver to see if there was any information available regarding Gary Thompson. He spoke to the constable who   the records department.

The constable told him that there were a few families with the last name of Thompson living in Vancouver, and he would need more about the Gary Thompson he was looking for to attain the data that Louis required. Louis told him what he knew about Gary and why he needed the information. The officer then told him that two events had recently occurred on the outskirts of Vancouver, like Louis's description of what happened to Jenna's husbands. He would try and get more information about the fellow named Thompson, and as soon as he had anything that might be helpful, he'd call him.

"Thank you," Louis said.

Louis didn't feel confident that he would get what he was looking for, *but something is better than nothing*, he thought.

* * *

Around the same time, Gunter was speaking with Ivan about arranging the special police team to infiltrate another building near Frankfurt, which was being watched by a surveillance crew. Some unusual activity had taken place in that building, as well. A dozen or so men dressed in black were seen entering and leaving at all hours of the night, bringing with them what appeared to be equipment of some sort. Strange lighting was seen flickering on and off inside the building and loud humming noises could be heard during the night. Some people in the surrounding areas had called the police department about these incidents.

Martin received a message requesting that the crew proceed to enter the building. He gave them the go-ahead. The team was quick in responding and stealthily moved toward the building. They were very organized in their efforts and careful not to cause any unnecessary disturbances before entering.

The leader of the team waved to four of his top swat men to move around to the front and the back of the building with the rest forming in twos and threes gathering around the rest of the structure. He gave the signal for them to go in. The team kicked the front door down and dashed inside the building. They surrounded a group of beings that didn't appear to be human.

One of them, seemingly the leader, raised a mechanical appearing hand. This action immediately halted the team from moving farther in. The leader's ears, or what appeared to be ears, were oversized, and there were peculiar lumps protruding from the side of its head. It was a giant among the other beings present.

Suddenly, mayhem broke loose. Gunshots were fired by the police team as they ran toward the leader and the other entities. Before the team could seize any of them, blazing light beams hit some of the front-line team members, paralyzing them on the spot.

Other members from the police team came up from the rear. They ran toward the robot-like beings, but they lost the ability to detain them and were compressed within a vapour like covering, which was emitted from some type of metallic cylinder. Standing within a gauzy shield, the leader spoke to the police team.

"We are here on earth for a specific assignment to change certain matters on your planet. We do not wish to cause humans harm. If you persist in your attempts to interfere with our mission, we will be forced to take drastic measures. Be forewarned now, before it is too late." With that said, all the beings vanished into thin air, and all their weapons and

technology in the room disappeared along with them. It was uncanny, as if nothing had been there in the first place.

The paralysis that some of the team members experienced dissipated after a few minutes, but everyone there was stunned. They couldn't believe what they had just witnessed. Even Martin, who entered just as the chaos began, was lost for words. There wasn't anything that he could express to ease the effect of what everyone had seen.

Martin positioned himself in the center of the room. "OK, men," he said, as the rest of the police team gathered around him. "It's clear we can't do any more right now. I'll arrange a meeting with all who are involved with trying to bring these attempts to an end. We need to come up with another plan. I never expected it to turn out the way it has."

"How can we possibly win?" Ivan asked, his voice rising. "It's obvious these aliens have much greater power than we have. From the looks of things, they could destroy us all with no effort, if they choose to do that," he stated, impassioned.

"Yes, it appears that way, but we must find another way to deal with these entities. I'm not sure how, at this moment. Perhaps, if we have enough people figuring out a way, together we might be able to at least deter them, if not stop them completely," Martin replied.

"What good would it do just to divert them from doing what they want to do? Didn't you hear what the leader said?" Gunter shouted out.

"I heard it," he said gravely to Gunter. "But we can't give up. We need to stick together and come up with a better plan to take these beings down."

"Personally, I think you're going to open Pandora's Box," Gunter continued to comment.

"There is that possibility. We can't allow these things to take over without some stronger efforts on our part." Martin exited the building, and everyone stood there in total confusion.

As the squad left the now empty building, some of the men continued to express themselves, stating that it was useless to even try to stop them; these entities were more powerful than any of them were.

CHAPTER THIRTY-THREE

Gunter needed to inform Louis about the latest event that happened at the building close to Frankfurt. He wasn't sure what it would mean for humankind. This alien assemblage had now become a major problem. Finding a solution to stop this invasion wasn't going to be an easy task. He promptly returned to his office to call Louis. He wasn't happy about the undertaking to try and stop these beings from taking over.

Louis's cell phone rang a few times before his voice mail answered.

"Hi, Louis, it's Gunter. Call me as soon as soon as you can. I have something important to discuss with you." He was about to hang up when he saw Louis's name come up on the display.

"Hi, Gunter. I was in the middle of another conversation when I noticed you called. So, what's going on?"

Gunter inhaled and exhaled. "You're not going like what I'm about to tell you." He then told Louis everything that had happened when the SWAT team infiltrated the secret organization's headquarters.

"Whoa! This is all far more than what I expected to hear," Louis exclaimed in disbelief. "None of that sounds good. How is getting a meeting arranged with everyone going to solve this huge, escalating problem?"

"It's beyond me, Louis. Martin seems to think that by getting everyone together, we might be able to brainstorm a greater plan and figure out how to get rid of these aliens once and for all."

"Do you really need me to be at the meeting? To be honest, I don't feel that it's going to help the situation. From what you're saying, these entities have a great deal more power available than what we humans have. They could annihilate the whole human race from the sounds of it."

"Jab, I know what you're saying. If you don't want to come to the next meeting to hear the solutions suggested, that's fine. I'm going to attend, though."

Louis vigorously rubbed the wrinkles on his forehead. *What do I do? Stay back or attend the meeting?* "Damn it, Gunter, you have put me in a sticky position."

"It's up to you what you decide," Gunter said, after Louis didn't respond for a moment.

"Let me think about it." Louis could feel himself becoming more and more stressed.

"Not a problem. Talk to you later." Gunter hung up.

As Louis hung up, he decided he wouldn't say too much to Jenna and Andrea regarding the latest episode. It would just make them more fearful. He would only say that the situation is still being considered. He hated to admit it, but deep down, he felt extreme concern. *What would it mean for all of humanity, if these aliens decided to take over the planet?* he thought.

Continuing with his inquiries about Gary seemed to be pointless, considering what he just learned. Nevertheless, curiosity got the best of him and he went ahead, anyway.

He called Gary's mother as he promised he would. "Hello Mrs. Thompson. This is Detective Cham beaux. I trust that all is well with you since the last time we spoke?"

"Yes, thank you. I feel a bit better now. Our last conversation was such a shock."

"Yes, I realized that, and I apologize for upsetting you. Would you be up for a meeting with me in about a weeks' time? I should in Vancouver by then; at least, I think I will be."

"Call before you come out here," Mrs. Thompson requested.

"Certainly, I will do that. As far as I know, I should be in Vancouver in the next week or so."

"Fine, Detective Chambeaux, I will expect your call."

Louis jotted down a reminder in his journal so he wouldn't forget to call her. He made another attempt to find out more about Brandon, but it was useless. It was always the same; no records of any financial transactions or past residences. However, one person he spoke with over the phone had some information about Brandon due to a clandestine meeting this person had with Brandon. He told Louis that Brandon was very secretive about what he did for a living. Anyone he knew that associated with Brandon, in any way, knew very little about him or anything that involved a family. It was then that Louis made the decision to quit searching for information about Brandon. It was time to call it a day on this guy. He called Gunter.

"Hi, Gunter, it's Louis. Has anything been arranged in regards to the meeting yet?"

"Ja. I just got off the phone with Martin. The meeting will be on Thursday of next week. A hall has been rented for us. What's happening with you?"

"I called Gary Thompson's mother in Vancouver to arrange a meeting w within the next few days. She's feeling better now and is willing to sit down with me and to go over things about her son. I tried again to get more information about Brandon, but each time, it's the same. I've discovered nothing more than I did through previous searches."

"Then, you know what, forget about him. It sounds like this guy is a dead-end for getting more data," Gunter remarked.

"My gut says he was involved with this secret organization, though. He must have changed his name over the course of many years so that no one could dig up any information on him."

"Yep, I think so."

"OK. I will continue with the meeting with Mrs. Thompson in Vancouver. Keep me posted about the meeting," Gunter. "Shall do, Louis. As soon as this meeting is done, I'll call you."

CHAPTER THIRTY-FOUR

The next few days went by quickly, and before Louis realized, it was time to arrange a flight to Vancouver to meet with Mrs. Thompson. More than anything, he was curious about Gary. The past few months of searching had been sheer frustration. He lost his momentum during his initial investigation on Gary after not being able to find much information on him, but he wanted to give it one last effort, and if he got no further ahead now, he would cease his search on Gary Thompson.

As soon as he got off the plane, he called Mrs. Thompson. She was ready to meet with him. He had lunch, then set off to see her.

Mrs. Thompson was anxiously waiting for him when there was a knock on the front door.

"Hello, Mrs. Thompson. How are you?" Louis greeted her as she let him in.

"I am alright, thanks. Please sit down," she said, guiding Louis into the living room. "Would you like a cup of tea or coffee before we begin?"

"A cup of coffee would be great," Louis accepted as he sat down on the couch.

While Mrs. Thompson prepared the coffee, he glanced around the living room. There was a picture of a young man sitting on the mantel. He assumed it was Gary, her son.

"Coffee is hot," she said as she placed a steaming mug in front of him. "Shall we begin? What is it that you wanted to know about Gary?"

"Is that a picture of Gary sitting on your mantel?" he asked, gesturing in the direction of the photo.

"Yes, that was taken a few years before he disappeared."

"I see." He paused for a moment. "How about you begin by telling me what he was like growing up?"

She told him that she and her husband had adopted Gary when he was two years old through an agency out of Labrador, Newfoundland.

"He wasn't very assertive in his communications, and he had difficulty making friends. She picked up a napkin, looking away for a moment before continuing. "He basically kept to himself, and neither I nor my husband could ever get him to speak about how he was feeling or what interested him the most."

"We always found that very strange, but he was our son and we accepted his oddities," she said, as she put her head down trying to hold the tears back. Slowly getting up from her chair, she walked toward the mantel and stared at Gary's photo for a few seconds. She then continued to say, "He moved out of our home in his twenties and moved around a fair bit. We never knew at any given point where he was living. Supposedly he had a job working for an environmental company in Alberta, at one point, but again, we really didn't know for sure. We never checked on his whereabouts. He was very private about his affairs. I guess we should have been more attentive."

"When did he disappear?" Louis asked.

"When he was in his thirties. We hadn't heard from him for a very long time. We tried to find him, but we had no luck. Then, one day, a police officer came to the house and told us that someone that Gary worked with called in and said he hadn't shown up for work for in over a week and were reporting Gary as missing. Gary apparently spoke about us to this co-worker of his, which seemed unusual for him to do. That's why the officer came to the house. He said they searched for him for a couple of weeks but they never found any trace of him.

"That must have been a horrible shock to you and your husband," Louis reflected.

Tears welled up as she said, "Oh! Believe me, we were devastated. For the longest time, we hoped that somehow through God's given grace, Gary would come home. After a few years . . . we just accepted the fact that he had died somewhere.

"I'm so sorry that you and your husband had to go through that experience. He was alive up until the year 2002. And from what I know, he was working when someone saw him fall to the ground. The man who found him called an ambulance and Gary was brought to the hospital, where he was pronounced dead."

"It all seems so strange." With tears welling up again, she continued. "I'm still having difficulty with the fact that he never got in touch with us in all those years . . . and then to find out that he was still alive, married, and died in Alberta not long ago. It saddens me so much, knowing that."

"It's quite understandable that you would feel the way you do. My colleagues and I think he was involved with a secret organization of some sort."

"A secret organization! What do you mean?" she asked, looking up at Louis in surprise.

"I'm not sure how to explain it to you. . ." Louise paused before continuing. "There's an organization called Nebula's Moon in Denmark. We believe Gary may have been a member of that establishment. This group wants to make changes here on Earth, changes which may not be in the best interest for mankind. And for all I and the other agents know, there may be similar groups in other areas of the globe looking to do the same."

"Oh, my lord!" she said, her face turning a grey colour. "Oh! My. This is worse than I could have ever imagined. What kind of changes?" she asked, feeling confused by what Louis said.

"The agencies are attempting to determine what those changes are. Unfortunately, it does explain why he didn't communicate with you all those years. His involvement with this organization probably meant that he had to sever all ties with his family and friends for whatever reason."

Mrs. Thompson sat on the chair with a look of despair on her face. She then got up and picked up Gary's picture again, staring at it for a few minutes. She turned to Louis, saying, "I will never fully comprehend the totality of what you have just told me. However, it does tell me to some degree why he chose not to contact us. It makes sense if this organization ordered him not to communicate with us, for as you say, whatever reason. How very sad," she said, while blowing her nose with a tissue.

"It is very sad." Louis stood up from the couch and shook Mrs. Thompson's hand. "Thank you for your time and for sharing your stories about Gary. It has helped me to understand things a little more clearly about your son."

"Are you and others looking to stop this organization from whatever it is they're planning on doing?" she asked as they walked toward the door.

"Yes, we are. I can assure you that there are efforts being made right now."

"Good luck, Detective Chambeaux. I hope it works out the way you want it to."

"Goodbye, Mrs. Thompson, and thank you for your help," Louis said, and he walked out the door.

Mrs. Thompson stood at the window waving goodbye. He turned to wave goodbye and noticed a look of great sadness on her face.

CHAPTER THIRTY-FIVE

While walking back to the rental car, Louis couldn't help feeling sad for Mrs. Thompson. How devastating it must be for her, hearing that her son had died. Now he had good reason to believe that his death may have been caused by the surreptitious organization that was being watched.

He would pass this information onto Gunter for his records and put the matter to rest. As he drove along the highway, Louis thought about everything that had happened so far during his investigation. Yet, it was by far the most spellbinding experience of his entire career.

Once he arrived at his hotel room, he arranged for a flight from Vancouver back to Paris. His was weary and felt the need to unwind before finishing his report. What he found out about Gary satisfied him, and he was confident it would shine some light on the situation regarding the unexplained missing and dead men.

* * *

The flight back to Paris was a safe and easy. Louis picked up his car at the airport parking lot and drove back to his apartment.

It was a long drive back from the airport to his office. Louis was hopeful that he could now slow down for a day or so. His visit to Vancouver had been mentally demanding. He wanted to fax his report to Gunter and Ivan, but there were some other papers he needed to pick up before faxing his most recent report.

It had gotten dark outside by the time he arrived at his apartment. He immediately noticed that the locked had been picked. There were scrapes on it that weren't there prior to his leaving for Vancouver. Quietly entering the apartment, he stood near the doorway for a few seconds; it was silent. "Hello, is there anyone here?" he asked out loud as he switched on the light. He was still on guard from the last episode, when he was almost run down and later found his hotel room ransacked.

Everything remained silent, and taking a deep breath, he tossed his briefcase onto the floor, took off his coat, undid his tie, and slumped down on the couch, feeling mentally drained.

It was too quiet. He clicked on the television just to have some background noise. He checked the phone for messages and saw that Gunter had called, but before returning his call, he wanted to have a beer. There was one bottle left in his fridge. After he finished it, he still didn't feel like talking. *It might be important, though*, he thought, and picked up the phone and dialed Gunter.

"Gunter speaking."

"Gunter, its Louis. You rang me at home, earlier?"

"Ja. I tried your cell phone. I couldn't get through for some reason, so I called your home number."

"That's weird. I didn't hear my cell phone ring. It might have been because I was still on the plane. Anyway, what's happening?"

"Just wanted to tell you that the meeting is being held on Thursday. I think it will be well attended. We have asked for outside assistance, and I think we will need it."

"That's good. Do you want me to be there?" Louis asked, hoping that he would not be necessary for him to fly back to Germany. Although he knew it would be an informative meeting, he felt tired to his bones. His muscles ached and dearly wanted to rest for a day or so.

"If you're up for it. I think it would be good to have you here. You might find it worthwhile. I understand that some of the outsiders have a lot of know-how regarding affairs of this nature."

"I hadn't planned on coming. But it does sound like it might be worthwhile. I'll need to arrange a flight if there is one available."

"If you can, great. If not, I will call you after the meeting to let you know the outcome."

"I'll see what I can do. I have a report for you, in any case. I was going to fax it to you, but going to the meeting and giving it to you in person might be better." He decided not to say anything to Gunter about his apartment lock being picked, thinking Gunter had enough to contend with now.

"Alright, let me know," Gunter said.

Louis hung up the phone. "Damn it!" he exclaimed out loud. "I wanted to kick back and relax for a day or so. I guess that's not going to happen now," he moaned.

He considered calling Jenna and Andrea to see how they were doing, but felt it best to wait until later when he was in a better frame of mind.

He called the airport to see if he could get a flight for the next day to Germany. Luckily, a flight was available. The flights seemed to be in his favour lately. He was beginning to feel like he had no place to call home these days, with all the travelling he had been doing. Still, it sounded like it was an important meeting, and he needed to pack some clothes and shave and shower before morning, so he got moving. The next morning, he struggled to get up, but making an exerted effort, he managed to get to the airport on time.

It was late October, and the days were starting to get colder and greyer in Germany. Louis enjoyed Germany in the summer months, but the colder months were not as pleasant. He sat at the window seat and gazed out at the cumulus grey clouds forming outside the plane. He then sat back and read his report over to make sure he had written everything down that Mrs. Thompson had told him. The more he read, the more he was sure that Gary was involved with the secret organization, Nebula's Moon, that the agents were investigating. *It will be interesting to see what information these new agents will have*, he thought, mentally preparing for what might be ahead.

CHAPTER THIRTY-SIX

As the plane flew toward Germany, there were some grave moments of turbulence occurring that made Louis nervous. It seemed to level off after a time, and the plane landed safely in Frankfurt.

It had grown colder, as he had expected. Louis wasn't particularly fond of the cold months, and he made sure he brought a warm parka with him. He rented a car at the airport and immediately headed to Gunter's office. He made a call while driving to let Gunter know he was on his way.

Gunter was preparing his presentation for the meeting when the call came through.

"Hi, Gunter. I'm on my way. I should be there shortly," Louis said, exhaling loudly.

"Wow! That was quick. I'm just cleaning up some things before the meeting. See you soon." Just as Gunter was ready to leave his office, Louis arrived, and they set off in the rented car.

Meanwhile, the agents from the outside perimeters of Germany were also on their way to the meeting. They needed to obtain the information they had attained about the secret organization and contacted the head spokesperson, Martin, beforehand. Martin was prepared for them. The agents didn't yet have the information he had attained.

The hall quickly filled up with German government officials, secret agents, detectives, reporters, clerics, and others who were interested in the affairs at hand. Martin would be introducing the people from outside of Germany to the audience.

After his introductory statement, Martin called upon a man who was from Frankfurt. The man gave a report on his data, as well as suggestions on how to best handle the growing problem of people unexpectedly disappearing. One of the more knowledgeable team officers had designed a great plan for apprehending the aliens, which would involve greater technology than what had been recently developed in Denmark, once they were certain they could seize these beings.

Gunter and Louis were surprised to hear this information. They had originally understood that the type of technology had not been developed in Denmark, but elsewhere.

After a few hours of discussion, debates, and suggestions, no strategies that satisfied much of the audience were proposed. Martin announced that they needed to take a break and resume after a lunch.

Gunter, Ivan, and Louis went together to have lunch at a local restaurant, which served great German food. The wiener snitchel was the best.

While they ate, the three men discussed the presentations that had been given that morning. Ivan was particularly impressed by the type of technology that had been developed. Even he didn't have any idea it was being industrialized in that part of the country.

Gunter was animated, gesturing with his hands while speaking in German. As Louis watched the two men speaking German, he felt somewhat left out. He understood some words, but not enough to participate in the conversation.

Everyone who attended the meeting congregated back at the hall after the lunch break.

It was getting to the most important part of the whole meeting. A highly recommended mechanical engineer from Denmark would be introducing the new technology. As the man brought out the device, there was complete silence from the audience. The apparatus appeared to be a cross between a laser and a machine gun, only larger than either.

The audience asked many questions, and as much as their questions were answered, many weren't satisfied with the process involving this technology, which would involve testing the equipment beforehand in one of the more rural areas of Frankfurt before apprehending the aliens. Heated discussions broke out throughout the room. The situation was getting out of hand, and Martin had to step in multiple times to stop the boisterous displays. The meeting had now advanced into a verbal fire pit.

As the meeting continued and the controversy flared, Ivan approached Martin and suggested that the meeting be postponed to another day. Some people were getting too volatile.

Martin agreed. He stepped up to the podium and explained that because the meeting wasn't going as well as he had hoped, it would be best to resume the following week.

"Ladies and gentlemen, may I have your attention. I had hoped that this meeting would bring about a solution to the situation at hand, but it seems there are some people here that are not happy at all about our intentions of using this technology to try and apprehend the aliens who are responsible for the attacks and the unexplained disappearance of people here and in different parts of the globe." And with that announcement, some shouted profanities toward him:

"You son-of-a-bitching bastard."

"You don't know what you're doing!"

Martin snapped. "Alright, that is enough. For those of you who want to see these actions stopped, we will the resume the meeting next week; otherwise, stay out of it." The meeting did not end on a good note.

It was then decided by the people in the audience that a vote should be put forth to see how many would be interested in continuing with the conference in a weeks' time. A few people didn't want to vote, and angrily walked out.

Gunter and Martin shook hands, calling it a day. The meeting was not as fruitful as they hoped it would be.

Louis asked Gunter to join him for a drink at a bar to talk about the proceedings.

CHAPTER THIRTY-SEVEN

By then, a month had gone by since Louis had left for Germany the second time. He had called Jenna and Andrea a couple of times, but with nothing much to add to the ongoing concerns.

Jenna needed to keep busy, and she made up her mind to look for a part-time job while staying with Andrea to help with the expenses. She answered an ad posted by an employment agency in the local newspaper; they were looking for someone to care for an older woman a few days per week. The job paid reasonably well, and she would only need to work, at the most, four days per week.

Andrea noticed that Jenna was beginning to act on edge again, and she thought it was a good idea for her to get a job. Within one week of answering the ad, Jenna was caring for the elderly woman. The job included making sure the woman was fed, bathed, and had whatever she required. The woman enjoyed reading books and often asked Jenna to read from some of the many books that were on her shelf. There were some intriguing books. Jenna was particularly fascinated by the books on paranormal occurrences; they made her think about her past experiences.

Jenna certainly found the job to be very different from anything she did in the past. She didn't complain at first; it kept her busy for a time and it provided her with some extra money.

However, after a month of doing this type of work, the job bored her. The work was not challenging enough, and she discussed her feelings with the supervisor who hired her. The supervisor told Jenna that it would probably be in her best interests to find something that would provide her with more of a challenge. Jenna resigned, apologizing for being unable to continue.

After she quit, she had more time on her hands again, and she began to feel restless. *It might be a good idea to go somewhere by myself for a time,* she thought. She knew how Andrea would react to this idea. Nevertheless, she made up her mind to take a break on her own. One evening during their dinner, Jenna decided to tell Andrea her plan.

"Andrea, I want to discuss something I have been thinking about with you. I need to have some alone time. I'm feeling jumpy for some reason, and I thought that maybe perhaps going somewhere by myself where it is calm would help me to simmer down."

"Are you crazy?" Andrea put her fork down and looked at Jenna, feeling fearful for her. "Going off by yourself like that! Nothing has been solved yet. Louis would have his say about this, I'm sure of it." She was clearly not open to Jenna's idea.

"I knew you would react this way," Jenna replied, feeling somewhat annoyed. "But I've made up my mind, whether you like my decision or not." Jenna stood up from the table for a few minutes, sternly looking at Andrea. "Nothing has been happening for some time, now. Maybe, these men, whoever they were, have stopped following me."

"Yeah, maybe, but what's to say they won't start following you again? Think about it more seriously, Jenna," Andrea said, feeling great uneasiness for her friend.

"I know you care about my welfare, and I appreciate it very much, but I need to have some alone time. That's not so much to ask, is it?" she asked, sitting back down on the chair.

"I don't know, Jenna. I would worry knowing you're off somewhere, all alone. You can be so stubborn at times," Andrea said as she walked to the kitchen to get a cup of coffee.

"Trust me that I'll be careful wherever I am."

"Where are, you planning to go?" Andrea asked, feeling frustrated with Jenna.

"I'm tossing around the idea of driving up to Lake LeClair in Alberta, where Brandon and I spent some time together. It's so peaceful and quiet there, and the lake is calming. I may take lessons on how to navigate a sailboat."

Andrea's eyes widened as she stared at Jenna, not fully understanding. "What! You can't be serious about this, Jenna!" she said.

"You have always maintained that I should let go of the past. What better way is there than by facing it head on?"

"Oh! Wow! I can't believe I'm hearing this. You're going to do this regardless what anyone says, aren't you?" At that point, Andrea was most upset.

Even though Jenna had made her up mind, she seemed awkward about it. "Yes, I am. Don't be angry with me. If I didn't feel a strong need to be by myself, I wouldn't argue with you. But I have to do this."

With a sigh of resignation, Andrea said, "Then there is nothing else I can say that will make you change your mind, is there? When are, you leaving?"

"I'm thinking Friday morning. That way, I'll have the whole weekend all to myself."

"Make sure you take your cell phone with you," Andrea added.

"Not to worry. I'll have with me wherever I go. I want to check and see what I've got to wear while I'm at the lake," she said as she left the room, ending the conversation.

Andrea couldn't help feeling great concern as she watched Jenna go to her room. Nonetheless, it was Jenna's choice, and she couldn't tell her not go.

CHAPTER THIRTY-EIGHT

Jenna called the resort where she would be staying ahead of time to reserve one of the cottages where she and Brandon had stayed a couple of times. She then asked Andrea if she would go shopping with her before she left on Friday. She wanted to buy some new clothes, especially a new bathing suit.

While shopping, Jenna found a great bikini, a couple of tops, shorts, and a lovely short sleeve yellow dress for going out to dinner in the evening.

"You made some nice choices. The dress is pretty," Andrea said, trying to dispel the fear she felt for Jenna.

"Thanks," Jenna replied, happy that Andrea was at least trying to be supportive.

By the time, Friday came around, Jenna was more than ready to get to the cottage. She put her luggage in the car and hugged Andrea goodbye. "Don't worry about me, Andrea. I'll be fine, honest. Maybe it would be best not to say anything to

Louis about my going to the lake. After all, I'll only be away for a few days."

Andrea, still feeling anxious, said, "I won't tell him if that is what you really want. Have a great time. Call me when you get there."

"I will, bye. See you in a couple of days." Jenna got into her car and anxiously drove off.

Andrea didn't have a good feeling at all about Jenna being on her own, especially at the lake. Staying at the lake where she and Brandon had spent some time together would surely invite sad memories for Jenna. Andrea was also concerned about the unsolved issues regarding the two characters who had followed her. These worries played on her mind as she walked back to her apartment. Andrea suddenly felt an unexplained sense of loss, but she brushed it off. There was nothing she could do; she had to accept Jenna's decision.

Jenna took her time driving to the cottage, enjoying the scenery along the way. She recalled that the lake was encapsulated within two mountains, providing a breathtaking backdrop. It was as if the mountains cradled the lake. Lush greenery flourished everywhere, and all kinds of wildlife scooted around the woods close by. She remembered it as being a serene place. Lake LeClair felt like a clear crystal in a sense. She always enjoyed being there.

There was a small general store on the grounds where Jenna could purchase some things if needed, and navigation lessons were also provided by the owners. Jenna was determined to learn how to navigate a sailboat.

She checked in at the desk and asked the clerk about the sailing lessons. They were booking for Sunday. The clerk could book her for Sunday morning early at around 8:00.

"Great, slot me in for 8:00 on Sunday. Do I require anything?" she asked.

"No, we have all the necessary items you need. I hope you will enjoy the lessons and the day."

"I'm sure I will," Jenna replied, smiling.

"You're in cottage 43," the clerk said handing her a key. "Turn left at the station and keep to your right."

"Thank you. I stayed in that same cottage a few years ago," she said, reminiscing.

Jenna couldn't wait to step inside the cottage. They were well maintained inside and out, as she recalled. The cottage that she booked was not huge, but for one person it was plenty. Excitement filled her. It had been a long while since she felt this thrilled about something.

She turned left, and there it was. It was everything Jenna remembered it to be: small, quaint, and delightful.

It was a serendipitous moment when she opened the door to the cottage. Memories flooded back of the first time she and Brandon were at the cottage. He picked her up before going in and placed her on the bed inside the cottage. The first thing they did was make passionate love, staying in for a long period.

There were other things she remembered, too, mainly about his behavior that seemed strange. She recalled how some of Brandon's traits were different from any of the other men she dated before him. He never really looked at her when they talked; he always looked to the side of her. It bothered her in the beginning of their relationship, but over time, she had accepted his odd mannerisms. She wasn't one for confrontation, and she didn't want to cause problems.

Brandon would leave without saying where he was going, and sometimes he'd be away for a couple hours at a time. Now, she wondered why she didn't question him about where he was or why he was away for so long. Was it because deep within her psyche she was afraid to know the reason? These were a few questions she hadn't considered before.

However, it was all in the past, and for her to move forward, Jenna needed to let it all go.

By the time, she had arrived, the sun began to set. It was a little late to go for a swim. She decided to go swimming in the morning.

She was getting hungry and thought to order in from a little restaurant down the road, located not far from the cottage. Brandon used to order take-out dinners from there at times. The food was good and reasonably priced.

She unpacked a few items—her bikini, a wrap and a towel—while she waited for her order to be delivered. They told her the food would arrive in about an hour. She then decided to go for a short stroll around the grounds to have a look at the scenery. Everything was in full bloom, and the air had a pleasant perfumed aroma about it. It was a scent that felt familiar to her from the past, but she thought, *it's just because everything is blossoming.*

After her walk, she called Andrea to let her know she had arrived safe and sound.

"Hello, this is Andrea."

"Hi. I made it here all in one piece. The cottage is small, but large enough for me. It's beautiful here with everything blossoming."

"I'm glad you arrived safely. It sounds nice. I hope the next few days will give you the peace and rest that you want," Andrea said, trying to make small talk to avoid mentioning how she still felt about Jenna being at the lake.

"I think it will. It's certainly quiet around here. There aren't too many people renting the other cottages right now, but that's OK. I want the quiet for a few days. Enjoy what time you have alone, too."

"I will. Call me later if you want."

"OK, talk soon."

Andrea felt unusually disconcerted about Jenna as she hung up, and wondered why she was feeling so out of sorts about her.

Jenna placed her cell phone on the sofa table and checked the cupboard for plates and cups; she found a place setting for four.

The take out arrived within the hour of her ordering. She thought a nice glass of wine would be nice, and opened a bottle of red cabernet to go with her meal. It happened to be one of Brandon's favourite wines.

She inserted a classical disk in the player, wanting to listen to music while she ate. It seemed too quiet. She hadn't experienced this kind of quiet for a very long time, and it felt a bit unsettling. The silence would take some getting used to. However, by that time her stomach was growling, and she woofed down every morsel of her dinner, forgetting about the uncomfortable silence.

Weariness began to take hold. It was time to settle in for the night. *Tomorrow will be a great day,* she thought, as she slipped under the bed covers and quickly fell asleep.

CHAPTER THIRTY-NINE

At the first crack of light the next morning, Jenna jumped out of bed feeling the best that she'd felt in a long time. For the first time in months she had slept through the whole night, not even getting up once to go to the bathroom. "Wow!" she said aloud. "I can't believe I didn't wake up during the night."

The sun was starting to beam through the bedroom window as Jenna looked out at the grounds. The birds were chirping and she could hear sounds from other critters scampering about the woods. "What a great way to begin my day," she exclaimed aloud.

In all her excitement, Jenna had forgotten to buy food. She decided to go to the general store to pick up some things. It supplied a few food items, which would suffice to quench her morning appetite. She decided to walk since it wasn't that far. The air felt different from the previous day somehow, and the sky was greying in spots. *Maybe rain is in the forecast for* *today, s*he thought. She hadn't checked the weather forecast. *Oh, darn anyway!*

No one else was in the store except for the clerk. "Good morning," Jenna greeted the clerk with a smile as she walked in the door. "Would you by chance have some eggs, onions, green peppers, bread, and coffee?"

"Yes, I do have all those things. I have a half-dozen eggs or one dozen. Bread and eggs are brought in daily, and coffee is instant. I only have one onion and one green pepper left, sorry."

"I'll take the half-dozen eggs, a loaf of bread, the onion, the pepper, and tea if you have any. I'm not fond of instant coffee."

"Yes, I have tea. Instant coffee is not to everyone's taste," the clerk agreed.

"Perfect." Jenna paid the clerk. "Thank you, and have a great day!"

"Same to you, Miss Paxton," the clerk waved as Jenna left the store.

Hurrying back to the cottage Jenna made a quick omelette with toast and tea. She was eager to finish her breakfast so that she could go for a swim, lie on the beach for a while, and then make some enquiries about the sailing lessons. She had decided that her time at the cottage would be spent at the beach and learning how to sail.

After she finished her breakfast, she placed the dishes in the sink, slipped on her bikini, grabbed her wrap and towel, and set out toward the beach.

Even though the sky above wasn't as bright and clear as it was the previous day, it was still nice enough to go for a short swim. Jenna gleefully jumped into the water. It was a bit cooler than she hoped, but tolerable. She saw no one else on the beach; it was probably still too early for most people.

While swimming, she gazed out toward the centre of the lake. The sky seemed to be getting darker in a certain area. She decided to take a break from swimming to lay on the beach for a half hour. The atmosphere seemed to be changing fast. Disappointed, she walked back to the cottage, thinking maybe the conditions would be nicer and clearer later in the day.

In the meantime, she wanted to check on the time for her sailing lessons and stopped in at the store. A good looking young man at the general store gave her the schedule.

"You are scheduled for tomorrow morning at 8:00," he said.

"What's your name?" she asked.

"My name is Joshua, please to meet you, Miss. . ."

"Oh sorry, I guess I should introduce myself, my name is Jenna Paxton. I used to come here a few years back. It's still as nice as it was back then," she said. She could feel her eyes filling up with tears as she thought about Brandon.

"Yes, it's a pretty nice place. I enjoy it here a lot." Joshua smiled.

"I hope the weather will be better tomorrow. Do you know what the forecast is saying?"

"As far as I know, it's supposed to be a beautiful, warm sunny day—great for sailing," he replied.

"Fantastic. Then I shall see you tomorrow morning. I'm looking forward to it."

"I think you will enjoy it," Joshua responded with a smile.

Jenna sauntered back to the cottage, and wondered, *now what will I do with my time?*

* * *

Back at her apartment, Andrea was beginning to feel overly unsettled about Jenna. She tried to keep her mind occupied by doing some cleaning, but thoughts and worries about Jenna kept interfering and getting stronger as the day went on.

"I'll call her to see how she is." But the phone rang and rang, and the only answer she got was Jenna's voice mail. "Hi Jenna," Andrea said, leaving a message. "I thought I'd give you a call and see how you're doing. I'll try again later."

Andrea was even more worried now that Jenna hadn't answered her phone. *Do I sit here and wait for her to return my call, or should I drive to the cottage?*" she wondered. The feelings stirring within her were too strong; something was compelling her to get to the cottage right away. She grabbed a few things to take with her, got into her car and speedily drove toward Lake LeClair.

CHAPTER FOURTY

Jenna paced around the cottage. She couldn't make up her mind about what she wanted to do with her day. She could either drive to the next town and have a look around, or stay indoors at the cottage and watch the few channels available on television. The weather wasn't co-operating like she hoped. After mulling it over, she opted to stay. *It's not so bad,* she thought, *I have my lessons tomorrow morning.*

The daylight had languished by the time she had made up her mind to stay at the cottage. There was enough food for the evening and the next day, and besides the fact that she wanted to do something, she felt that settling in for the night was the better of the two options. Jenna surfed through the few channels and chose an old classic movie to watch. Her stay at the cottage was not as exciting as she had initially thought it would be, but there was not much else for her to do until she had her lesson the next morning.

A sudden unexpected loneliness swept over her. "Come on, Jenna, what is the matter with you? This is what you wanted, stop this right now!" she said aloud. "Oh, great! Now I'm talking to myself. I'm losing it." She turned to the movie and tried to pay attention, attempting to distract herself from her feelings of loneliness.

After the movie ended, she poured another glass of wine and sat down, surfing through the channels once again. Nothing on television caught her interest and she decided to go to bed early.

As she slept that night, she dreamt that she was lost in a deep fog and was unable to find her way out. It was as if the fog kept pulling her in. She woke up panic-stricken in the middle of the night, but feeling extremely tired, she fell back asleep.

* *

Jenna awakened the next morning feeling better, but a part of her felt slightly out of balance, and she wondered if it was caused by the dream she had; she couldn't remember what it was about.

The sun was rising, and the sky looked clear. She was looking forward to her lesson that morning. She made a quick breakfast, showered, and by 7:45 she was ready, giving her some time to check out the harbour and the boat before the lesson started. As she waited near the edge of the dock, the young man named Joshua walked toward her.

"Good morning, Miss Paxton," he said as he approached her with a toothy smile. "Are you ready for your lesson?"

"Indeed, I am," she replied, excited to be starting.

"OK, hop on and we'll get started."

Jenna was eager to begin and was quick to climb on the boat. Joshua showed her how to check all the sails, tighten the rigging, and perform the other important steps that needed to be taken before sailing. Then he slowly navigated the sailboat through the waterway onto the lake.

While they sailed, Joshua explained to Jenna how to properly steer the sailboat and gave her some tips about sailing. She was ecstatic. They sailed for a couple of hours, and she thoroughly enjoyed it, wanting to do it again soon.

"You did great for the first time," Joshua commented as the lesson ended. "You just have to fine tune your skills a little more, that's all."

"Thank you so much, it was fun!" Jenna replied, feeling refreshed from being on the water.

"Anytime, Miss Paxton. Just let me know if you'd like another lesson. So long for now."

"Bye, and thanks again." She was glad she had decided on taking sailing lessons.

By the time the lesson ended, it was time for lunch. She wanted to walk to the edge of the pier after having lunch to sit for a while and enjoy the quietude.

Her immediate thoughts were of Andrea. *Maybe I should give her a ring.* But then she realized she left her phone at the cottage. *That's not very smart,* she thought. She strolled back to the cottage and saw that Andrea had left a message. She called her, but there was no answer. She didn't leave a message, thinking she'd try her again later.

Jenna needed to do something and decided to go for a long walk along the beach and have a gander at the sailboat she had been on, thinking that maybe a boat might be something she could purchase at some point in time. She truly enjoyed being at the helm.

As she began to walk, a single dark cloud began to form at the end of the pier. *That's odd*, she thought. The sky up until that very moment had been clear and bright. Suddenly, a dark haze arose, and everything around her became eerily still; not even seagulls flew overhead. The water, which generally flowed gently against the beach's edge, stopped moving completely as though frozen in time. Trying to focus more precisely on the dark mass, she moved down the pier to get a closer view of it. It appeared to be moving toward her as she moved closer, and it seemed to be getting bigger the closer she got. Surrounding the black mass were rippling pockets of energetic vibrations, pulsating in and out. Then a tunnel opened within the darkest patch. It contracted and expanded like a lightning stream, and from within a tunnel, a form appeared and walked toward her. Jenna couldn't believe what she was seeing. It was Gary, beckoning her to come with him. Trembling like a leaf, she screamed, "No . . . No . . .! Go away, go away! This isn't real!"

"Jenna, it's me, Gary," the apparition of Gary said in an obscure tone. "Come with me. There is a better place for you. Brandon is here, too; he wants to speak with you."

Shrieking, she said. "No, don't do this to me!" She backed away, repeating it over and over.

Again, in a dulled tone, Gary said, "Listen to me. I am here to take you to your new home. Remember this." He threw her the gold chain that he had given her for her birthday one year. Frightened and confused, she examined the chain with puzzlement. "Oh, my God! It's the same one he gave me. I don't understand! Someone, please, help me!" she yelled, but there was no one else around.

Feeling faint, she staggered, almost falling. A sudden beam of light flashed through her body, making her regain stability. Then two men in black garments came forth from the black mass and stood on either side of Gary. Brandon stood behind him. On the right side of their garments was the insignia she had seen on the button that she found at the Louvre in Paris.

Brandon then spoke. "Gary and I and my comrades here can explain everything to you. But you must come with us. There isn't much time left. Trust me. It will all be explained. Please, it's time."

Tears flowing, Jenna screamed, "Stop this, please! No, go away."

* * *

In the meantime, Andrea had arrived and checked in at the reception desk. The clerk informed Andrea that Jenna was last seen near the pier. Panicking, Andrea ran as fast as possible toward the harbour.

As Andrea neared, Jenna was being pulled into the black miasma. Andrea saw a figure that appeared to be Gary. "Jenna, no!" she yelled. "No, don't go! Please, listen to me, he's not real!"

Jenna turned toward Andrea with a gaze so unworldly, so unexpected. Her eyes glowed red for a few seconds. Gary then grasped Jenna's hand and together they stepped into a tunnel in the black mass, and all vanished before Andrea's eyes.

Andrea stood at the edge of the pier in shock. Tears rolled down her cheeks like a waterfall. For several minutes, she could barely stand; it was all so unfathomable. *How can this be happening?* She questioned over and over, not understanding what had just happened.

The tears just wouldn't stop. The more Andrea thought about the uncanny event while driving back to her apartment that night, the more rattled she felt. She had never been so shaken. It was an experience she couldn't begin to explain; it was unreal.

CHAPTER FOURTY-ONE

It took Andrea several weeks before she felt like she was beginning to feel like her normal self. The incident at the lake had been the most devastating and enigmatic experience of her entire life. She wanted the memory of it to go away. Recognizing that Jenna was gone and that she would never see her again was a harsh reality.

She felt it was important to inform Louis about the uncanny experience she had. *He'll have a difficult time believing it, though*, she thought. *But he should know.*

The last time Jenna had spoken to Louis, he was still in Germany. Andrea could locate his current whereabouts by making a call to the detective agency in Paris. They gave her the phone number where he could be reached. She was hesitant at first, and her hand shook as she dialed his number.

"Louis, it's Andrea. I have bad news."

"Oh! Now what's happened? Is it Jenna?" Louis asked with concern in his voice.

"Yes, it has to do with Jenna. You're not going to believe what I'm about to tell you," she said, pausing for a few seconds.

"It doesn't sound good from the tone of your voice." Louis suddenly felt like something foreboding awaited him.

"You might want to brace yourself," she said. She then told him everything that had materialized since he had returned to Germany.

Louis's throat momentarily seized up; he couldn't form the words that he wanted to say. It was as though he was hearing a story from a science fiction novel.

Stammering, he replied, "Andrea, I . . . don't know what to say. There are no words that will ease the loss of your best friend. I believe you, but I don't think anyone else will believe you if you plan on sharing this story. My suggestion to you is to close that door and leave it closed. Too much has gone unsolved with this affair, and from what you've just told me, the story is totally off the wall. There are people that would see it that way. They wouldn't believe you."

"I know you're right Louis. I've thought about it over and over, and I have decided to keep it to myself. I also know you had strong feelings for her."

"So, you figured it out." Louis said, with some resignation in his voice. He hadn't realized that Andrea had noticed his actions around Jenna when he was in her company.

"It wasn't hard to figure out, Louis. It's too bad you never told her how you felt."

"I know, tell me something I don't know." He replied, feeling less than OK with the fact that he never told Jenna how he felt about her.

"It's going to be a long time before I can forget about this horrific twist of fate for Jenna. Frankly, I don't know if I ever will forget it, and I still sometimes think it didn't happen. I just had to tell you."

"The event probably will always be at the back of your mind, Andrea, and you will feel that way, but you have to move on with your own life. Pray that wherever she is, Jenna has found the happiness and the love that she always wanted," Louis responded, feeling despondent.

"I have. Believe me, I have, and I will keep on praying. What's this going to mean for you?" Andrea asked. "I'll have to inform a good friend of mine who works as an undercover agent in Hamburg about this uncanny event. I'm sure he'll find it difficult to believe, but I know he'll keep on doing what he's supposed to do regarding the events that have occurred in the different areas of Germany, the Netherlands, and other locations around the globe, especially once he knows about this bizarre occurrence."

"I wish you the best, and good luck with your endeavours in finding out the truth. Keep in touch, if you can. Goodbye."

"Goodbye, Andrea. Take good care of yourself." Louis put the phone down as though it were a rock.

He needed some time to get his thoughts together before speaking with Gunter about this episode. He already knew what Gunter would say.

* * *

The investigations into Nebula's Moon continued, even though Gunter knew what had happened to Jenna. He wasn't one hundred percent sure about it all, but he was also aware that there had been a lot of strange incidents, which carried no viable explanations, and he wasn't about to give up searching for the truth.

The black SUV that was used to try and run Louis down was eventually found. It had been abandoned on a country road outside Frankfurt. No evidence of any kind indicated an alien was responsible. The agency found out that someone stole it from a car dealership outside of Hamburg during the night.

As for the special police units tracking down any other unusual circumstances, they continued with their efforts. However, they still hadn't been able to obtain enough solid proof to halt the organization they suspected was behind all the attacks. The mystery continued to be an ongoing affair.

Louis returned to Paris from Germany for a much-needed break.

While back in Paris, he decided to write a book about the mysterious occurrences that he had become involved with over the past several months. He particularly wanted to write Jenna's story. There was so much to write about; where would he begin?

Due to the stress of everything that had gone on, he started smoking—a bad habit he'd given up several years ago, He wasn't at all pleased with himself that he had picked up the ghastly habit again.

As he sat in his darkened office blowing smoke circles, he thought a lot about Jenna. It wasn't often in his career that he had developed strong feelings for a client; she was one of two in all his 25 years of working as a detective. He very much regretted not telling Jenna how he really felt about her.

"We just never know what life has in store for us. It's too late now, isn't it Louis," he said out loud, berating his non-action. He'd never forget what he experienced for as long as he shall live, and he would never ever forget Jenna.

One day several months after Jenna's inexplicable exit, out of curiosity, Louis decided to travel to Lake LeClair to have a look around. He wanted to see for himself the place where it all ended for Jenna. Or . . . was it a new beginning?